1140 Productions

Slave to the Game

Catt Hamlin

Brandon McKinnie is a former division-one athlete turned entertainer and writer. Basketball was his first love before discovering his talents and love for storytelling. He has starred in and written several projects made for television, film, stage, and new media. And it is his pleasure to now add author to his list of gifts from God.

"YOU EITHER CHANGE THE GAME, OR BECOME A SLAVE TO IT."

BRANDON MCKINNIE

1140 PRODUCTIONS

Published by 1140 Productions
1140 Productions, LLC, www.1140productions.com

Published in the United States of America by 1140 Productions, LLC 2020

McKinnie, Brandon
    Slave to the game with Richard Gray

ISBN: 978-1-7344200-0-5 (pbk)
ISBN: 978-1-7344200-1-2 (electronic)
ISBN: 978-1-7344200-2-9 (audio)

Library of Congress Control Number: 2020905439

To the village that raised me.

Table of Contents

FOREWORD

I started out as a below average Computer Science major at Chicago State University. Imagine that. Today, for better or for worse, I work on the management side of my own agency where I guide the careers of professional basketball players – both during and beyond their playing days. The bridge between Chicago State and where I sit today as I prepare this foreword is the epitome of being a "slave to the game." We were never driven by a destination or an outcome. It was a chase after a round ball, and all the memories and different places and things that we had the pleasure to experience in the process were all incidental.

We skipped out on different types of extracurricular activities, family functions, and exploring different paths in life that were available to us so that we could play the game from sunup to sundown because we were "slaves to the game."

They told us the odds of making it to the highest level was one to several hundred million, but we ignored it because we were "slaves to the game."

This book and my contribution are both products of being a "slave to the game." The author, my brother of almost 20 years, has been telling this story for the past 5 years, and the possibility of it all coming together is because he is a "slave to the game."

We need it. We yearn it. The game has a gravitational pull like none other. It will drive you to do things beyond imagination, during and beyond the game. So, while this story will expose some of the flaws associated with the game, the overarching message is that the game is a vehicle of empowerment and opportunity, even if it is misguided at times.

I'm a proud "slave to the game."

PREFACE

Slave to the Game was derived from many conversations in the barbershop with my mans, Shanks, about what it would be like if all these star-studded athletes would attend HBCUs instead of the high major colleges. From those conversations, I decided to write the screenplay. Took me a year or so to get it done but once I did, I knew I had something special. But getting a movie made in Hollywood is sometimes like trying to find a needle in a haystack.

So after a year of just sitting on the project and folks telling me it was dope, the idea of the book was conceived. I wanted this story to get out there no matter what in hopes that it will create awareness for the subject matter as well as create a brand for the project. While I hope to sell millions of copies, the goal has always been to make this project into a movie.

Since writing *Slave to The Game*, it seems that the subject of Black star athletes attending HBCUs has become more prevalent than ever. We've had a couple of these kids take visits to HBCUs, celebrities and athletes have been openly talking about it, and Black media have been using their platforms to write articles and discuss it on air. All this was telling me that time was of the essence and that I needed to get my version out—NOW!

Though basketball is the angle this story is told from, I'd like to think that this story is more than a sports story and not just for the fans of sports. It's a story of legacy and strength and acknowledgement of one's self worth. And anyone can do anything if they put their mind to it.

Nothing changes, if nothing changes. We all have the power to make changes for the better, even if it means being the first to do it. After all, somebody has to be the first. Why not let it be YOU!!

Chapter 1 – The Plan

*A*nd *with a minute and ten seconds remaining in the Illinois Boys' State Championship, Simeon has a chance to take the lead,"* the commentator enthusiastically calls into the mic. *"Crossing over…and WHAM! After a ten-point halftime deficit, the Duke-bound superstar confidently puts his team up by two with less than a minute to go!"*

The six-foot-four-inch, tall and lanky framed, Rick Gray, the nation's number two recruit in the ESPN Top One Hundred, winks at Sir Walker as he trots backwards up the court. Sir, a slim but chiseled, six-foot-three-inch point guard and the nation's top recruit, ignores Rick's showboating and claps for the ball, emphatically demanding it from his teammate. Sir brings the ball up the court, skillfully shaking his defender, making a screeching sound with his sneakers on the court's surface with each change of direction. He glances up at the clock while his coach yells out the play. The stadium's crowd, packed to a capacity of 16,000, stand to their feet roaring thunderously, some yelling, "Defense!" while others chant, "Let's Go!" as they cheer along with the cheerleaders, optimistically shaking their poms. Players and coaches alike from each of their respective benches are on the edge of their seats or gripping towels as the seconds go down on the clock. Sir blocks it all out, only hearing Coach Griffin yell, "SIXTY-TWO-HIGH! SIXTY-TWO-HIGH!"

"Calling up the play, Walker looks to set it up," the announcer commentates. From the top of the key, Sir puts a move on the defender. One of Sir's teammates comes off a screen, open and waving for him to pass the ball, but Sir looks him off.

"PASS THE BALL!" Coach Griffin yells from the sideline.

"Walker shakes the defender, stepping back…"

Sir shoots, more confident in himself than he is his teammate.

SWISH!

"He nails it! Jordan Prep leads by one!"

Simeon's coach signals Gray to call for a timeout. The whistle blows with a score of 60-59 and 37 seconds left in the game.

"And Simeon's coach wants to talk it over."

As Sir crosses the court towards his team's bench, he glances into the stands to find Percy Daniels, arms folded glaring down at him with a look of intrigue. Sir felt torn – thoughts of choosing what he wanted versus what was best for him and his family raced through his mind. Coming from a young, single—mother—home, Percy was like a father figure to Sir and had been there for him throughout his entire basketball career. The times when his mom would've struggled to keep the lights on while in nursing school, it was Percy who made sure the electric bill was paid and kept the heat on in the cold winters of Chicago. Even still, Percy asked more of Sir than he had the capacity to handle at the age of eighteen. He walks to the bench to see his coach also looking at him but with disappointment from his shot selection.

"What was that, Walker?" Coach Griffin demanded.

"Coach, it went in," Sir responded flatly, taking a seat on the bench.

Just then, Howard University's new young basketball coach, Corey Bradford burst in from the cold through the stadium's entrance and hands the usher his ticket.

"You know the game's almost over, right?" the usher insists.

"Better late than never," Bradford exhales, out of breath, before running to find a spot to stand inside the arena.

Sir is at the bench, huddled with his team as his coach goes over the play on his clipboard. Sir can't help but see Percy still peering down at him from across the court in the stands.

"If we trap right here, guaranteed we'll come up with the steal on the cross-court pass, so be ready. Sir, you ready?"

"Yeah," Sir, says only half hearing his coach. "Yeah, Coach. I got it."

"Defense on three!" yells Coach Griffin as the team puts their hands in the middle of the huddle. "One…Two…Three…"

"DEFENSE," the team responds in unison.

Sir looks in the stands behind the team to see his mother, Joy. She directs praying hands and a bright smile his way. He lightens a bit, giving her a half smile in return.

"And it comes down to this as Jordan Prep and Simeon take the court for the final seconds of what has been a thrilling ball game."

On the court, Sir and Rick focus in on one another. Simeon is to inbound the ball. With the defense on the balls of their feet and their arms stretched, the clock ticks away as Rick brings the ball up the court. He sets up the play and passes the ball with twenty seconds left.

"Gray sets it up. It's passed around."

Sir watches as Rick cuts through the lane and then out to the corner. Rick gets the ball back.

"Gray is open in the corner."

The Jordan Prep players trap Rick the way their coach instructed them to.

"As Jordan Prep sends the trap..."

Forced to pass, Rick throws the ball before falling out of bounds.

"Gray looks for help and it's deflected! Walker has it! He's ahead of the pack with a lone defender ahead of him!"

As the crowd roars, Sir races ahead of everyone up the court. Percy's piercing eyes key in on Sir. He hesitates.

"Walker slows down. NO, he proceeds."

With a full head of steam, Sir drives to the basket. The lone defender stands between him and the rim.

"Jordan Prep has a two-on-one advantage."

With five seconds in the game, Sir goes up in the air.

"Walker keeps it. He goes up…"

With the confidence of every game he's ever won, Sir soars in the air knowing he's going to land a rim-shaking dunk.

"It's blocked!"

Sir falls, not feeling the pain of his body smacking against the court. He looks up at the clock as the defender recovers the ball and hauls it down the court.

"Garner recovers it! Three seconds! He heaves it down the court."

The ball moves as if in slow motion through the air, barely grazing the fingers of Jordan Prep's last line of defense and then lands in Rick's hands.

"Gray catches it…"

Sir watches from a recumbent position as Rick slams the ball in the basket, adding two points to the scoreboard just as the clock hits triple zeros. The buzzer sounds, ending the game.

"SIMEON WINS! SIMEON WINS!"

Simeon players and fans flood the court in excitement.

"Oh, my goodness. What an ending!"

Sir, still on the floor, looks up at Percy who smirks condescendingly before walking away. He then looks over at his mother's sympathizing eyes before he drops his head in defeat.

"The lingering question, I'm sure everyone wants to know is, what would possess Sir Walker to shoot the ball instead of just holding it and waiting for the foul?"

In the locker room, most of the players have gotten dressed and have left with their families. The few that remain, hang their heads—trying to hide tears and frustration. Among them still is Coach Griffin and Sir, siting stone-faced, highly disappointed in himself.

"Come on, fellas. Hell of a season," Griff says.

"We'd be the state champions if KD over there wasn't trying to play hero ball," shoots one of Sir's teammates.

"Hero ball? Y'all wouldn't even be here if it wasn't for me!" he shoots back.

"We wouldn't be losers if it weren't for you either, bruh!"

They banter back and forth a few rounds before Coach Griffin steps in. "All right, all right. Everybody just calm down. Emotions are high right now. It takes a team to win, and it takes a team to lose. If you want to blame anyone, blame yourselves. Blame me. But don't go around pointing fingers at each other thinking it'll make you feel any less like crap. Tomorrow is a new day."

"I guess when you're the star player, you still get your ass kissed no matter how selfish you are," Sir's teammate barks as he grabs his bag, exiting with the remaining few.

Coach Griffin places his hand on Sir's shoulder. "You're a great player, Sir. But you're even a better person. And I personally know that you always try to make the right choice. So, hang your head high despite losing today. And allow me to thank you for entrusting your talents with me these past four years. Now, come on, let's get out of here."

"You can go ahead coach. I'll see you out there."

Coach Griffin and Sir's bond is like one of a teenaged parent having his first child, in the sense that they grew up together. Like a parent learns how to be a parent after becoming a parent and not a moment before, Coach Griffin learned how to be a coach when he was introduced to Sir. And though one was older and responsible for the growth of the other, it was more of a student-student relationship than a teacher-student relationship. Coach Griffin, as a first-year inexperienced high school coach, was fortunate to be graced with a talent such as Sir's. They learned from each other. They developed each other. And they pushed each other to be great in their own rights. And just like in every parent-child relationship, the child has to leave at some point to find his way. And now it is time to go their separate ways.

As Sir entered into what would normally be a hallway full of people, after purposely lingering in the locker room, he is grateful to see that it is fairly empty, except for Percy, who is approaching and Coach Bradford standing there in a Howard Basketball polo, holding his coat and patiently waiting on Sir, like a kid awaiting to see his favorite celebrity. "Hey Sir, do you have a minute?" asking, with his hand extended.

Sir sighs, not really wanting to be bothered but also not wanting to be rude. He hasn't made a decision yet about any school and doesn't feel like talking about it or the game.

"I'm sorry, Mister, but I'm not trying to do any interviews right now," he says mistaking him for a reporter.

Corey laughs, "No, I'm Corey Bradford, the head basketball Coach at Howard University." He pulls out his card, extending it. It's intercepted by the hand of Percy, flossing an iced-out Breitling watch. This catches Corey by surprise.

"I'm sorry, you are?"

"Percy, Sir's… Handler," he says with a devilish grin.

"Okay, well I'm…"

"Oh, I know who you are," reading the card, "You're Corey Bradford, head men's basketball coach of Howard University."

This wouldn't be the first time Sir has heard of Coach Bradford. Although he doesn't follow Howard basketball, he recalls the name from the multitude of recruitment letters that Coach Bradford has personally sent him over the past year, which was shocking to him because every coach that has sent him a recruitment letter in the past two years has been nothing short of a high-major program – Duke, UNC, Kentucky, etc. The other programs would consider it a waste of their time and money to go after a player of Sir's caliber, but here Coach Bradford is in the flesh, standing in this hallway. Sir appreciated the persistency.

"I don't want to take up too much of your time, especially after such a tough loss."

"Then don't," Percy interjects. "This is the number one recruit in the country. What makes you think that *we* would even consider playing for the likes of an HBCU?" Before giving him a chance to respond he says, "Good night Coach Bradford. Sir and I have a long trip back to the city. Come on, Sir, let's roll." Sir looks at Coach Bradford one last time, sighs, then, proceeds with Percy.

As Percy and Sir take off down the hallway, Percy throws his arms around Sir's shoulders, "By the way, we did good tonight."

"Sir, P… slow up," Rick yells, entering the hallway from behind them. "No love for the champ?" Sir pulls away from Percy, rolls his eyes in the back of his head and puts on a more cheerful front, turning to see Rick on one knee holding up the number one with his finger. "Sir, remember this pose, boy!" Rick says smiling from ear to ear.

"8th Grade City Champs, Bryn Mawr Grammar School," Percy interrupts. "Y'all had the city on lock. A better question is, do y'all remember the plan?"

Slightly frustrated, Sir replies, "Nah Percy, what plan was that?"

"The two best 8th grade guards in the city, going to separate powerhouse high schools, in separate classes," Percy says, then pauses, exchanging stares with Sir and Rick. "Both walking away as state champs."

"Oh, I definitely remember, P," Rick responds. "Blame this guy. He's the one who got all touchy-feely about the new STEM school and skipped out on Bogan at the last minute, and we see how that worked out."

"Yeah," Sir shoots. "McDonald's All-American and the number one player in the country."

"And state champ, runner up," Rick says, pointing to his state championship hat and shirt.

"Listen, enough." Percy interrupts the two brothers at heart and grips them both by the shoulder. "So, we got a little off track. But we're still behind the wheel. You both are All-Americans, and Sir will pick a college in a separate power conference, and we can still control the NCAA like we planned to do in high school." Percy glances at Sir. "As long as we stay on track, and we don't deviate from the plan, we all will win next time. Got it?"

Sir snatches away and sees his mom waiting in the stands. "Yo, congrats bro," Sir says mildly. "It's your moment and I'm happy for you. I'll get you next time… champ. I'm out."

They both let out a light in-sync laugh with a hug. Sir gives Percy a halfhearted handshake and shoulder hug then walks toward his mom.

"With you staying out of it, I honestly thought he was gonna get me on this one. I know how bad he wanted one," Rick says to Percy in a low tone, feeling for his brother's loss.

Eyes locked on Sir walking away, Percy replies, "It's okay, he'll be fine."

After a five-hour drive from Peoria, Illinois of mostly flat grass fields and farmland, to their home in big city Chicago, Sir and his mother arrive in the wee hours of the night. Sir walks into his bedroom tossing his gym bag on the floor, then plops down on his bed. He stops in his tracks, scanning the walls of his room and sighs heavily. He looks at the 8th grade championship photo of himself and Rick, the basketball trophies, Jr. Olympics medals, City and AAU championships, plaques, ribbons, certificates but no state championships. It became overwhelmingly clear to him there never would be one.

Ready to wash the night away, he undressed and got in the shower. Sir usually played music while he bathed but tonight, he just let the sounds of the hot water running on his face be his soundtrack. Unable to drown out his thoughts, his entire athletic career up to this point flashed through his mind—his first basketball camp, the years of squeaking gym shoes across the court, the buzzers before half time... the thoughts were endless. It seemed as if every whistle ever blown in a game were playing in his mind. The more Sir thought, the harder he scrubbed his body. His caramel-colored skin reddened under the pressure of the loofah vigorously rubbing against it. He tried, but he couldn't wash away the grime of the loss.

After putting on his night clothes—a pair of basketball shorts and a cutoff tee—Sir grabbed his phone and plugged it into the charger next to his bed. He began to scroll down on the home screen to see the numerous missed calls, texts, tweets, ESPN, Instagram and Snapchat notifications. Instead of opening any of them, he turns his phone on *Do Not Disturb* and places it face down. Lying in bed and feeling no better, his body wafts with the emotion of the finality of the game. *Damn.* All the work he's put in over the years for it to all amount to a state championship game that he'd lost.

Joy lightly knocks on the door before entering. The light taps of her small footsteps were sounds Sir became accustomed to hearing over the years as his mother came to kiss him goodnight.

"You sleep, baby?"

Sir lies still, barely breathing, afraid that if he spoke two words to his mother, he'd drown them both in his tears.

"I just want you to know that you're a champion in my eyes. Mommy loves you, Boo." Joy kisses Sir on the temple, knowing he was awake the entire time. She turns off his light and closes the door. Once he is certain she is in her room, Sir exhales and lets the tears stream down his cheeks.

The next morning, Sir awakens to the aroma of sweet, buttery pancakes, eggs and bacon, along with the sound of his mother going over cue cards as she makes breakfast.

"A complete or partial collapse of the entire lung or area of the lung is… Atelectasis?" Joy contemplates before opening her textbook to check her answer. "YES!" She pumps her fist as she's seen her son do so many times over the years.

Sir, dressed in a Fashion Geek hoodie sweat suit and ready for school, watches his mother in awe from the kitchen entrance. He can tell that she is tired, but her bright face makes even the heaviest of under-eye bags seem light on her face. "Smells good," he says, as he walks into the kitchen, grabbing a piece of bacon.

"Test today, right?" he asks as he kisses her on the cheek.

"Baby, when you're studying to be an RN, it seems like there's a test every day."

"You got it, Mama."

"You know I do!" she says assuredly as she sets a plate of food in front of Sir. "You know, Coach Cal called. Coach Williams, Boeheim, Izzo, and about hundred others," she exaggerates. "Everybody wants me to give you their support. You doing okay, Boo? You didn't say much in the car on the way home."

"Yeah, Mama. You know… It is what it is."

Not wanting to push, Joy makes a silly face, causing her son to smile. She looks at the clock and takes the apron from around her waist.

"Okay, Baby. I have to go. I won't see you tonight, I picked up a shift at the restaurant. Have a good day at school. Love you!" she says before kissing him on the cheek and running to the door with her book bag and purse.

"Love you too, Mom! And good luck on your test today!" he yells out after her.

"Thanks, Boo!"

Chapter 2 – Shop Talk

Prince Jones Barbershop is a small, storefront barbershop located in Prince George County, Maryland—better known as PG County— just about ten miles from the Howard University campus. Since the 1960's every chair was typically occupied here no matter the day, and no one was ever in a rush to leave. It is a weekly routine for men to come get a haircut and talk *shop* from sports to dope fiend family members to religion. Nothing is off limits. The four African American barbers, ages ranging from thirty to sixty-five, are the source for the latest news around the country, but they specialize in the news and history of PG County and its surrounding areas.

This is where Coach Bradford has been coming to get his hair cut and let his coat hang since landing the head coaching job last spring. Prince Jones Barbershop reminded him of the shop he frequented growing up in Chicago. And after playing junior college ball in a small town outside of Oklahoma, then division two in Colorado, then being an assistant coach in the cities of Kansas City, Des Moines, and Bloomington, where he met his wife, this shop felt like a home away from home. The men of Prince Jones Barbershop are proud of the young coach and want to see him succeed. And the way they talk basketball to him, you would think they are on his coaching staff.

"COACH!" they all yelled out as Coach Bradford walks through the shop's door, into a brightly lit shop, accented by black artists' paintings from Justin Bua and Ernie Barnes.

"How was your trip last weekend?" a barber asks.

"Did you sign him?" another asks.

Coach Bradford places his hand on the back his head then rubbing it over the crown to his forehead, "Well, first, my flight was delayed several hours," Coach Bradford tells the barbershop. "Then, I got to the game with about half a minute left. Then, I waited about two hours after the game to talk to him, just for his 'handler'," he air quotes, "to pull Sir away from me without me saying as much as who I was. Waste of trip if you ask me."

"So, you didn't sign him?" his barber jokingly says as he snaps the cape around Coach Bradford's neck.

"Yeah, I signed him all right. To a no-words-exchanged, very non-verbal commitment."

"What's the boy's street agent name?"

"Percy."

"PERCY!? Sound like something you catch on your feet!" a barber jokingly says, creating laughter in the shop.

Pops, the shop's hefty gray-bearded owner and eldest barber chimes in, while applying shaving cream to a patron's face, "I knew a Percy once. Used to run numbers. A bad boy he was. Knew how to make things happen in the city. Definitely not a guy you wanted to cross. He the reason I see any other guys named Percy, I crosses the street. Them Percy's ain't no joke, Jack!"

A patron jokingly shouts, "Man, you probably owe him some money, Pops. That's why you really crossing them streets."

Pops laughs, "Man go-head on. Money, that's what that boy street agent wants."

"Yeah cause he definitely, taking care of that kid."

"He probably the reason that boy threw that game."

Surprised, Coach Bradford says, "Wait, what? Who threw what game?"

"That's right. You missed most of the game. Your boy look like he was out there point shaving big time. Comes out after the half, up ten points, and starts taking all kinds of ill-advised shots. Then he gone shoot that shot at the end, when everybody and they momma know he should've just held the ball and taken the foul, went to the line and hit two free-throws. Bang. Bang. Game basically over. But nah, this dude..."

This is all news to Coach Bradford, as he sits there listening to the shop chime in with their various opinions on what happened.

Then a barber yells out, "Coach B, I know you're a standup guy and all but uh, you want a chance at Sir Walker, you're gonna need somebody at Howard to give you a bag for him. Straight up."

"Sir Walker?" Pops says. "I wonder is he any kin' to Aldis 'Sir' Walker?" He was from Chicago, too. Played for Howard when I was coming up. Aldis was a baaad boy! Aldis would come down the court, give you one of these..." Pops imitates his best Aldis Walker move. "and that was all she wrote. You hear me, Jack?"

"Yeah, Aldis was a bad boy. Had the sweetest shot, too," the other older barber confirms.

While the barbers and patrons of the shop talk about the who's who of the basketball world, and who could do what and who did what better, Coach Bradford can't help but sit there and wonder if there's a connection to Aldis and Sir. And if so, what is it? And how could it help him in recruiting Sir?

Chapter 3 – Booney

A week following the state championship game, it's five in the morning and Sir is running drills alone while blasting music with a small personal speaker connected to the Bluetooth on his phone. Even though he knew he was the only one of his peers up, he keeps his phone on Do Not Disturb so as not to be distracted by notifications on his phone while practicing. Sir jumps up for twenty quick off-the-backboard passes to himself, making sure to stay light on his feet before dunking the ball at number twenty-one. He dribbles up the court as if he has a defender. He shakes his imaginary defender to the left, and then to the right, dribbles the ball between his legs before sinking a three-point swish at the top of the key. After running a few more dribbling drills, Sir racks the basketballs and practices defense. He stays low to the ground, shuffling short bursts of speed with is arms out on either side—forcing his imaginary opponent to change direction. Once his legs are good and burnt out, Sir grabs a ball from the rack. He dribbles from the top of the key and leaps up to make the same dunk that was blocked in the championship game. He repeats the same dunk over and over until his eyes burn with both sweat and tears.

"Hey, kid!" Booney, the school's engineer yells from the other side of the court. "Give yourself a break, a'ight?" before disappearing back into the hallway.

Sir could only see the blurred profile of Booney across the court, but he welcomed the gentle tone he grew used to hearing over the past four years. Taking his advice, Sir racked the ball and gathered his things before going into the locker room to shower and get ready for school. Going to the gym early had been Sir's routine since freshman year. Practicing alone was his therapy. No distractions—just basketball.

After getting ready for school, Sir sits on the bleachers and scrolls through his various social media accounts. Mid-swipe on his timeline, an incoming call from Percy pops up on his screen. Instead of letting it ring like he has done over the past week, he pressed *Ignore* and continued scrolling on his phone. He scrolls to an ESPN post with his photo that says, "The nation's top high school player still undecided." He sucks his teeth and keeps scrolling. He double taps a sneaker head post and a few pictures of his cute classmates he never had time to pay much attention to outside of class. As he scrolls, he stops at a post that reads: "Howard Bound" and taps it to see a video of an excited vibrant teenager gripping her acceptance letter.

"Y'all see this! Do y'all see this? A scholarship to Howard, baby! Ayyye! I'm about to go to the same school Diddy went to! That's cold. I might be the female Diddy y'all!" She exclaims.

Sir smiles at the enthusiastic teen and taps on the "@Howard1867" tag in her caption. He scrolls through the university's page and sees an array of Black students, professors, and celebrities all going hard for the university. He stops at clips of the band at football and basketball games where students are amped in the student section. The distinguished fraternities and beautiful women in sororities catch his attention before he stops at a candid photo of Coach Bradford coaching from the sideline at a basketball game. He had to give it to him. The man had guts to approach him and Percy, even if just for a moment. Sir knew when people saw him, they saw money, whether for their university or their program. To actually believe an HBCU basketball program had a shot at having him enroll, was

unheard of and ballsy.

Booney comes in the gym dropping his toolbox next to the

basketball rack and swoops up a ball. Sir smiles and puts his left thumb on

the post, so his timeline doesn't refresh.

"He shakes left! He moves right! Spin move! He…" Booney

zealously narrates before throwing up a complete air-ball. "Damn. That used

to be my go-to move. The crowd used to go wild when I'd hit 'em with

that."

Booney had been Jordan Prep's engineer since its inception four

years ago when Sir arrived. He was in his late forties and had once been a

ball player himself. He had earned himself a scholarship to the University of

Maryland before opting to leave the university when he found out his, now,

wife was pregnant. He's seen and even matched up against some of the best

players from the city like Isaiah Thomas, Benji Wilson, Tim Hardaway,

Quentin Richardson, Dwayne Wade and more, but none like Sir. Sir was

special in Booney's eyes. Booney is a student of the game and can recite

stats of those who'd played in Chicago since before he was born. Like many others in the city, Booney is inspired when he watches Sir play. Sir reminds him of himself in how hard he worked, except Sir was much more talented on the court as he would always let him know.

Booney is the one who left the school's door open for Sir in the mornings so that he can work on his game, sometimes even before those early morning Coach Griffin practices or the free personal training sessions that are allotted him by guys hoping he'll use their paid services once he makes it to the NBA. The two of them talk about basketball more than a Jeff Van Gundy and Mark Jackson commentating at an NBA game. Though many years apart in age, they are on the same level with their knowledge of the game. No disrespect to Booney. Sir looks up to Booney and considers him one of the most genuine figures in his life, in a sense that he had nothing to gain from Sir's success. Therefore, Sir trusts and confides in him greatly. But not even Booney knows where Sir was headed to play next year.

"What up, Big Homie!" Sir calls out as Booney comes in for a handshake.

"I can't call it, young Sir. What's up with you? Haven't seen you in here since the loss. You good? How you holdin' up?" Booney sincerely asks.

"I'm alright man, it was a hard loss, ya know?"

"Yeah, you can't win 'em all. Of course, I was rooting for you. Man, I thought you had it. But you got that McDonald's game comin' up in a few days, huh? You excited?"

"A little bit. Been waiting on it my whole life. Just not thrilled about all the questions about where I'm gonna play next year, ya know?"

"Still undecided, huh? You got time. What you got there?" Booney asks, pointing to the screen. Sir's thumb is still pressed to in his left hand.

"Oh, this? Just a school I was checking out on the 'Gram. Some female got accepted and is super excited so I was just checkin' it out," turning his phone so Booney can see.

"Howard U! What you know about that?"

"Nothing, really. I know it's an HBCU and that my grandfather went there back in the day. But that's about it."

"That's right. Aldis was a Bison, huh?"

"I guess. The coach there sent me a few letters and was at the championship game. So, I figure I'll check them out since I came across them."

"Howard's a good school! Great education. Caring professors. The livest parties. The baddest sistas go there. And it's one of the top HBCUs in the country."

"Dang, Boon, you sound like a commercial for them!" Sir jokes.

Booney laughs, "I guess I do."

"You wanna know something funny? I don't even know what an HBCU is. I just know it has to do with a college for black people."

"That's exactly what it is, young Sir, Historically Black Colleges and Universities. There are at least a hundred of them throughout the country. They used to be the only schools that black folk could attend back in the day. That's probably why your grandfather went there. It sure wasn't many choices for them."

"Word?" Sir inquires, never considering that was the case. "That's messed up. I heard he was really good too, till he blew his knee."

"Yeah, Aldis was nice. As a kid, I saw him play a few times. He was the you of his time. But of course, he wouldn't have been able to attend a Kentucky or Duke cause they weren't really giving Blacks those types of opportunities back then."

"That's terrible."

"Not so much as when the top Black athletes finally got a chance to attend the Kentuckies and the Kansases of the world, they… well, *we* forgot about the HBCUs that were there for us first."

"Man… money changes everything," Sir says, thinking about the choices he's made because of it.

"Sure does," Booney replies. "Once the big boys got a whiff of our true value, it was all she wrote. And lack of knowledge about the history and quality of the education is what we weren't taught. So HBCUs started losing us because they definitely couldn't compete with the facilities and exposure that the others could offer. TV contracts and what not. Hell, even I didn't understand an HBCU's value to our people and our community when I was coming out. But I soon found out. And the only thing that HBCUs don't have are players like you attending them. Imagine that though, McDonald's

All-Americans at HBCUs! They'd be on TV with big shoe contracts and winning championships. And Duke... Duke would just be another school with a good med program."

Universities had been looking at Sir since he was in the seventh grade, but he never put much thought into it beyond what Percy wanted. He always thought the rules of the NBA would have changed by now and he'd go straight from high school. So, the thought of choosing a university, which entails more than just basketball, feels like too much pressure for Sir. All he really cares about is taking care of his mother and playing ball. To be honest, he doesn't care where he plays as long as he gets to compete. He understands his talent and is not concerned about the name on the front of his jersey, as evident by the high school he chose.

"...You know, I just thought about something, kid. You could've went to any powerhouse high school in Chicago, but you chose little ol' Jordan Prep with a first-year coach and program at the time. And you led them to the championship. You ain't win but you did lead them. That was a power move. Just like LeBron James taking his talents to South Beach and back to Cleveland, Dr. Dre leaving Death Row and like Dave Chappelle walking away from fifty million dollars." He rethinks about Dave Chappelle, "That might've been a little crazy at the time, but nonetheless, it was a power move. Those moves said, 'You don't own me. Not you, not basketball, not your school, not your team, not your contract or your company. I own me, not you!' And those are the things people remember most. Even more important, it's what people respect, young Sir."

"Man, ain't nobody gonna respect me if I go to an HBCU though!"

"You're wrong kid. The world will respect you! And, it'll change college basketball as we know it. Let me tell you something. Something I learned after my days of playing were over." Booney leans in closer to Sir. "You either change the game, or you become a slave to it."

Before Sir could respond, a woman's voice comes over Booney's walkie-talkie asking him to come to the cafeteria.

"Here I come, sweetness," he says into the walkie-talkie.

"Boy, you better stop," the woman's voice giggles back."

"If I wasn't a happily married man, that Ms. Johnson would be in trouble. You hear me? I'll see you later." Dapping up Sir, Booney walks off.

He picks up another basketball and sinks an easy lay-up. "I still got it! I'ma holler at you, young Sir."

After pondering for a brief moment, "Hey Booney," Sir grabs his bag and jogs up behind him. "How you know the sisters are bad up at Howard? You never told me you went there too?"

"Nah, but my wife did. And my daughter graduates from there in May. Don't get no badder than that, kid."

"High key," Sir says smiling.

Later that night, Sir is home on the couch, spinning and toying with the basketball as he watches ESPN. The analyst reports, *"Since the end of the season they've already indicted several agents, college coaches and representatives from shoe companies that are tied to a conspiracy ring linked to providing impermissible benefits to top high school talent. There is an ongoing investigation that is said will pull the cover off of a corrupt underworld in amateur athletics, blowing the lid on several top university programs."* Sir's stomach sinks at the thought of his relationship with Percy being exposed to the level of what is currently going on in the

NCAA. And like clockwork, Percy's name pops up on his phone. Sir, while appreciative of Percy being somewhat of a father figure, experiences a mixture of guilt, irritation and anger towards Percy and it's wearing on their relationship by the minute—one ignored call after the next. He wonders why things have to be so complicated but then reflects on his conversation with Booney about using basketball to change the game and making a power move. The same can apply to his relationship with Percy.

Sir stares at the ball in his hands, thinking about all the accolades, experiences, triumphs and failures he's endured so far, all because of this piece of leather. He then begins to drift into a reminiscent daze of the night he and Rick first met Percy:

A younger Sir and Rick are pacing down the sidewalk of a dimly lit street, fresh off a win at the fifth and sixth grade league at the Jackson Park Community Center during the summertime when this area of Southside Chicago is more chaotic than usual. Holding a basketball and carrying a gym bag won't give them their typical pass from conflict with the gangs in the neighborhood, so they walk urgently toward the bus stop.

"Man, bro, why'd you do those boys like that?" Sir says, laughing. "I wanted to embarrass them as much as you did, but if embarrassing them a little less could get us home safer, it's ok to take it a little light at the end. Hezzy, between his legs to the floater? Too much, bro!"

"You know me, bro," Rick replies confidently. "It's kill or be killed. But who does a Shamgod, then shoots an NBA three in a real game? Yeah that's taking it lightly alright."

"Yeah, I guess you do gotta point," Sir says, mimicking the move he did in the game.

A silver Benz with dark, tinted windows pulls to the curb just behind them, slowly following. The driver flicks its bright headlights, appearing to want the boys' attention.

"Yo, who that?" Rick asks.

"I don't know, man," Sir says, fearfully. "Whoever it is, don't make no eye contact and keep walking."

The car picks up speed, now driving alongside them. The passenger side window slowly comes down. A man donning a disingenuous smile lays eyes on the boys.

"What up, young fellas," the man says. "Hell of a show y'all put on in the gym tonight."

"Keep walking and don't look over there," Sir says under his breath.

Sir and Rick pick up the pace, eyes glued straight ahead. Their first thought is to break out and run but running down a damn near pitch black street could do more harm than good in a neighborhood known for violence. Sir can hear his mom's voice in his head preaching to him about going to random neighborhoods to play ball.

"Come on fellas, I ain't gonna harm y'all."

The driver throws the car in park and jumps out of the car. He trots over to cut Sir and Rick off their path, holding up his hands, showing he's unarmed to keep them calm. "I'm a fan," he says as the boys slowly stop walking. "I've seen some great ball players come through these Chicago streets, D. Rose, Bobby Simmons, Will Bynum... you name it. With the confidence and skill you boys have at such a young age, you could be next."

More easily impressed than Sir, Rick's eyes widened. "You for real?" Rick says. "Those some legends you talkin' about, man. Thanks!"

"Just calling it like I see it. I'm Percy," he says, extending his fist to be bumped.

Frantically extending his fist, "I'm Rick and this my boy, Sir. We bout to take the city over."

"I'm sure y'all are! Nice to meet you, little man." He then reaches his fist in Sir's direction. Sir is hesitant. He makes deep eye contact and feels the man out a little longer before finally giving in and bumping Percy's fist.

"Nice to meet you too, Percy. We need to get out of here. Can't miss our bus."

"You sure you boys don't need a ride? Where you from?" Percy probes.

"Nah, we're good," Sir says authoritatively. "We can't be just jumping in cars like that."

Rick nudges Sir out of sight knowing that a ride would definitely be better than standing on the bus stop. "I mean, Sir's mom would like it if we were home sooner than later, I'm sure." Sir cuts his eyes at Rick, *WTF?!*

Understanding Sir's hesitancy, "Check it, at least sit in my car and wait for your bus to get here," Percy suggests.

They look around and there isn't a bus in sight.

"Deal," Rick says. "Ain't no harm in that," as he walks toward the car with no sign of approval from Sir. This wasn't up for debate. Sir shakes his head in disgust. "And, we from over east. Bryn Mawr, baby!" Rick exclaims.

Frustrated, Sir snaps back, "Could you yell that any louder? This ain't a Bryn Mawr neighborhood, in case you forgot."

Percy laughs, "I like you two already. Sir, trust me, my car is the safest place you can be on this side of town. When your bus gets here, you can take off. I just want to make sure you boys are safe."

Sir nods and follows Rick to the car. Percy smiles.

Rick gets in the front seat of the car and Sir in the back. "This car is crazy," Rick says, amazed at the woodgrain and chrome interior finish. "What kind is it?"

"It's a Benz. S550," Percy replies. "So, talk to me. Where you shorties learn to ball like that?"

"What you mean?" Rick asks. "There is a lot of cold hoopers in Chicago."

Percy laughs. "Y'all really don't know. What I saw in there was special. Sure, there are talented kids in every neighborhood in the city, but the way you guys carry yourself... your attitude." Percy exchanges eye contact between Sir and Rick. "There's a maturity about your games that will ensure that you will always make it to the next level. As long as you keep the right people around you."

Sir, following along, is not sure what to make of the strange man that seemed to appear out of thin air. "Let me guess, the right people mean you, right?" He asks.

"Peep it, fellas," Percy continues. "I'm what you call a hoop historian in Chicago. I'm known in every gym in the city from Jackson Park, to Whitney Young, to DePaul and the United Center. I love the game and I appreciate youngsters like yourselves that take your craft seriously. I knew you weren't from around here, and the way y'all handled those boys in there, they didn't take that too kindly, so I just wanted to make sure you were good."

"You have to excuse my boy, Sir, he be bugging sometime," Rick says, causing Sir to cut his eyes at him yet again.

"I get it. I understand. And I like it," Percy replies. "Always stick together, look after each other, and don't take anything from no one."

Sir sees their bus approaching and begins to grab his ball and gym bag. "Well, our bus is coming, so we better go." Sir says.

"Indeed, you do. Get home safe, and I'll see y'all around." Percy gives them both a firm handshake as they exit his car. Feeling something in the palm of Percy's hand, Sir pulls away to find five crisp and folded up twenty-dollar bills.

"What's this for?" Sir asks, scrunching his face.

"A performance like y'all put on deserves pay."

"Nah, we cool," Sir says, handing the bills back in Percy's direction.

"No, we ain't," Rick interjects with his eyes widened while snatching the bread from Sir's fingers. "Thanks, Percy! Let's roll, our bus is 'bout to pull off," Rick exclaims, jumping out of Percy's whip.

Sitting a few seats away from the driver, across from each other in the seats facing the aisle, Rick toys with the money in his pocket Percy gave them, while Sir glances out of the window, eyes locked in on the houses, gas stations and well-lit liquor stores as the bus speeds along. This time of night, the buses are mostly empty, and since the boys haven't said a word since boarding, they can hear each other's thoughts as if that is a thing.

"What was all of that about?" Sir finally says, breaking the silence.

"What you mean?"

"The way you were acting with that Percy guy. Acting all giddy like you know him. He could've kidnapped us, shot us and threw us in the lake for all we know."

"Man, he wasn't gonna do nothin'. He seemed cool to me."

"And then you take that dude's money?" Sir continues. "What you owe him for that, now?"

"Like he said, we should be getting paid for the way we balled out. Besides, we can both use the money. I'm staying with you because we ain't got no electricity right now and y'all's refrigerator didn't look too full when we left this morning, so…" Rick shrugs.

"I'm just saying…" Sir hesitates. "When people I just met are extra friendly and trying to give me stuff, it seems iffy to me."

"Iffy or not. Free money is free money. And I'm hungry."

Sir lets out a sigh, pondering about the potential consequences of the strange gift. But Rick was right, they hadn't eaten in the past eight hours. "Yeah, I feel you... So, I guess we ordering a pizza when we get to the crib then?"

"Italian Fiesta on deck!"

They both laugh and slap hands as the bus comes to a stop. There is an outburst of loud noises and rude playful chatter as six teens a little older than Sir and Rick enter from the rear doors of the bus. Knowing the young men didn't pay their fare, the bus driver glances at them through his rearview mirror and decides that ignoring it would be the best way to handle it. Whether caused by intimidation or fatigue, he doesn't bother and keeps driving. The teens move closer to the front of the bus where Rick and Sir are and sit in the seats immediately behind them. Rick and Sir make swift eye contact. Aware that anything could erupt at this point, Rick slips the money they just got from Percy down the front of his boxer briefs.

A voice emerges from the small talk among the group of teens, "Where y'all from?" The bus goes silent. Sir and Rick weren't quite in their neighborhood yet, so a question like that could lead to some major problems.

"We from the city bro," Rick reluctantly replies. "We don't want no problems."

"You not from around here though," the taller, heavy-set teens says. "And I ain't your bro." He gets up and plops down next to Rick.

Sir stands and attempts to stop things from getting any more out of hand, "Look, we just coming from playing some ball. We don't gang bang and we headed to the crib. Our stop is close."

"That ain't how it works," the heavy-set one says reaching his hands toward Rick's pocket. Rick slaps his hand away and instantly stands shoulder-to-shoulder with Sir, their fists clenched backing their way closer to the front door. This isn't the first time Rick and Sir had to fight their way out of a situation being typical for kids growing up in Chicago having to navigate through multiple neighborhoods.

The brakes of the bus slam. "ALL YOU KIDS OFF THIS BUS!" the driver yells. Sir and Rick run off first with the teens high on their heels, exiting right behind them. As the teens close in on Sir and Rick down the dark street, a car speeds past the bus and pulls over in their path. A man jumps out in front of the teens, hand clutching the inside of his pocket as if he has a gun. They stop in their tracks. Rick and Sir's hearts are in their throats. They turn around to recognize the familiar car and the tall, lean stature of the man. It's Percy. With his hand in his pocket, staring down the teens, he signals Rick and Sir to get in the car. Rick jumps in first. Sir, less doubtful and more grateful for Percy than before, quickly follows.

"I think you fellas better leave these two alone and head the other way," Percy says calmly.

The teen who stood in front of the pack bucks back instantly, "This ain't your problem, joe. We don't recognize them, and we can't get caught slippin' by nobody we don't know riding around our way."

"They're shorties," Percy replies. "They ain't about any of that. So, I'll say it again. You should probably head back up the block." The teens return eye contact, not backing down. To not confuse this exchange as a plea for cooperation, Percy pulls the gun out his inner pocket and cocks it, then points it at them. Sir and Rick duck down in the back seat of the car as the teens break for their lives down the block. Percy tucks his burner, looks around to see who could be watching then jumps in the car.

"Percy, man... thank you," Rick says, slightly hyperventilating. "Where did you come from?"

"I followed the bus," Percy says with a straight face.

"So, you knew?" Sir asks.

"I know Chicago. Two kids from the east side on a bus from Jackson Park? That's a different gang every few stops. I guess your street IQ ain't caught up to your basketball IQ."

"Man, we appreciate you looking out," Sir says.

"Like I said earlier, I just want to make sure you guys are good, so don't sweat it." Percy says, weaving through traffic and glancing at the boys in the rear view. "Where am I taking you guys?"

"Sir's crib, 75th and Yates."

"Oh, y'all are from the eastside for real," Percy says. "Had those guys known you were from over there, that wouldn't have ended well. Can't move around all reckless like that, you know?"

"Yeah, we just want to ball." Sir replies. "If they say the run is good, we in there. We want to play against the best, no matter where it is." Rick nods his head in agreement.

"I hear you youngin'," Percy says with an approving smirk. "I like the spirit, but you have to be smart about it and live to see everything play out. Y'all heard of Ben Wilson, right?

"Who Benji?" Rick exclaims. "You know it! Number one player in the nation. Who doesn't know him?"

"And what else?" Percy asks.

"Killed the day before the start of the season of his senior year," Sir replies.

"Right, so you know your history," Percy says. "If he had a chance at a do over, the stuff that happened that led up to his murder, he'd rethink it. You little dudes just dodged a bullet. You never know what would've happened if I didn't follow that bus. Use it as a lesson." Percy's car pulls up in front of Sir's home—a middle income, 3 story apartment building. Appears to be well taken care of. His grandfather passed it down to his mother. It means everything to their family.

"This it?" Percy asks.

"Yup, this is us," Rick responds.

"Oh, you live here too?"

"For a little while," Rick answers. "Percy, thanks again, man. You're a life saver—literally."

"Yeah, thanks," Sir chimes in. The boys jump out of the car. The front porch light comes on. The door flings open, and Sir's mother storms out to the front porch.

"Sir, Rick... Is that you?" She yells from the porch. "I was worried sick about y'all!" Wearing only a robe on top of her pajamas and her house shoes, she walks off the porch toward Percy's car. "Whose car is this?" She asks. "Start explaining!"

"Ma, chill!" Sir says.

"Don't tell me to chill. I told y'all about going off to these areas alone and staying until late. It's bad enough you're going in the first place. And who is this man?"

Percy rolls his window down. Turns on his calm, charming demeanor. "Miss," Percy says. "I can explain everything, if you'll allow me." Sliding his gun under his seat out of her sight, Percy exits the car and approaches Joy with a friendly hand extended. "I'm Percy, Miss. Please, if I could come in and explain, you'd feel better about everything."

Questioning whether or not she could trust this strange, well put together man, she stares at his extended arm before eventually shaking his hand. She insisted that Sir and Rick head in immediately and then pointed Percy toward the door. "Make it quick," she says.

From that day on, Percy was a regular in Rick and Sir's lives as well as their families'. Like he promised that day in Sir's living room, whatever they needed, he took care of them, but it came with a price. Sir is ready to be free from it all. He just wants to play ball, get to the highest level and make sure his mom is good. That's it. Playing ball is the only plan, and anything that threatens that is in the way.

Joy breaks Sir's train of thought when she peeks her head in, "Hey, Boo, am I taking you to the airport in the morning or is Percy?

He quickly responds, "Nah, you are... Please?"

Taken aback by his sense of urgency, "Oh, okay. Are me and him on the same flight going out there?"

"I'm not even sure if he's going. For the time being, it's just us."

She can tell that his behavior is off but decides to digress, "Okay, Boo. Have a good night. Don't stay up too late watching TV."

"I won't. Hey, Momma?"

"Yeah, Boo?"

"Do you think if Papa could've gone to Duke or maybe Kentucky, he would have chosen a bigger school instead of going to Howard?"

"You know, I can't really say but I doubt it. He always talked about his great days there. I heard him once say that if it were up to him, both his kids would've been Howard alum." She stopped to think for a second, "You know, your Uncle James got in, but he chose to go to the military instead. Broke your grandfather's heart."

"What about you, Ma?"

She smiles and says, "Actually, baby, I got into their nursing program. But I found out I was pregnant with this beautiful baby boy and knew moving to Washington DC with him wasn't an option at eighteen. So, I started working and made sure we were good."

"I'm proud of you, Momma. I really appreciate all you've sacrificed. I'm gonna make it up to you for sure."

"You know something, I'm proud of me too." They both laugh as she winks at him before walking out.

Chapter 4 – Mickey D's

With a pair of Dre Beats headphones wrapped around their necks, Sir and Rick carry their Nike Elite backpacks through the bustle of the Hartsfield-Jackson Airport in Atlanta. A cameraman and videographer pace ahead of them, taking photos and filming their arrival when a group of kids run up to them.

"Sir, can I take a snap with you!?" one of the kids asks.

"Of course, you can little bro. Let's do it," Sir says as he throws his arms around the kid and striking a silly pose. The two players take turns signing autographs and taking selfies with fans.

"We've come a long way boy," Rick says giving Sir a playful shove.

"Sure have! Our first time here was for the AAU nationals in like sixth grade.

"Yep," Rick says laughing. "except it wasn't on no plane. Eleven of us crammed in Percy's van. Only you and me could get the front seat and the middle seat with the leg room."

"Word," Sir replies with a deflated chuckle. "Had to protect his primary investments."

"Bro, what's the deal with your energy toward P? We been like a family for as long as I can remember. You've been bugging a little since the exchange after the state championship game. He do something wrong? He said you skipped out on the ride with us to the airport with no explanation."

"Nope, we all good," Sir replies, choosing not to expose his true feelings towards Percy. "It's just a lot to deal with."

"I feel you," Rick says. "But it doesn't seem like you're tryin' to make it any easier on yourself coming down here undecided on your school choice. You about to be bombarded with the same questions for the next four days, —'Where do you see yourself going?' 'When do you plan on deciding? Blah, blah, blah. They gonna wear you out, my guy."

"Yeah, I know right, but it'll all be over soon."

Posing for one last photo, "Well while you're focused on answering questions about what college you're going to, I'll be concentrating on winning the McDonald's game MVP." Rick says, smiling. "I'll take that off your plate. One less thing for you to worry about."

"Come on, bruh, now you know that's all me." They both laugh together and continue walking as they see Earl Singleton walking toward them.

"But seriously, let's make it right with P, whatever it is," Rick pleads. "He gets in town tomorrow and wants to take us to dinner one of the nights while we here to discuss things."

"I'll let you know," Sir says dismissively. "Big Earl! The preacher man's son himself. What up big fellal!"

Earl flashes a bright smile, complementing the shining gold cross chain around his neck. He reaches out to both men, dapping them up with his mitts for hands and hugging them warmly. Big Earl is the fifth ranked player in the nation according to ESPN. He stands at six-feet-ten-inches and weighs in at around two hundred forty-five pounds of natural country-bred strength. He's a big teddy bear with a warm smile. Not a very outspoken person—just likes to let his game speak for him.

"I see you got some new bling, big fella. Your father's church must be saving a whole lot of lives," jokes Rick.

"Yessir! The church is growing every day! God is good! But Lord knows I'm ready to finally get up out of Dallas for good. This trip to Atlanta is much needed. I can't wait 'til I graduate."

The boys continue to joke and chatter as they make their way through the airport and arrive at the pickup area where they are greeted by a driver in a black SUV.

"We VIP status I see," Rick says, as he tosses his bag in the back of the truck. "This is about to be the norm real soon."

"High-key," says Big Earl. "I pray I don't lose my mind in the process."

"May the good Lord guide you," Sir jokes. "But high-key, we've been celebrities in our own right since forever cause of social media. Big fella, when your EYBL summer mixtape dropped last summer, you had the whole world tweeting about your size and skills. It almost broke the internet. I mean look at my messages!" Sir flips out his phone and continues. "Look at all of these DMs, comments and likes. It's the norm already."

"Yeah, but you also complain about how you wish you can shut it all down cause it gets overwhelming," Earl replies snatching Sir's phone.

"Man, you have a thousand unread messages! You got the celebrity part down pat, Mr. Hollywood. Rick, get your boy!"

"I already know. No cap, he can't wait to start acting brand new," Rick jokes as he and Earl share a laugh.

"Peter is Facetiming you," Earl says.

"My favorite shooter!" Sir exclaims. "Answer it."

"Ahem, you mean your favorite shooter not named Rick," Rick interjects.

"Oh, now you jealous," Sir says in a playful tone. "You know you're my first, my last, my everything." The guys break out in laughter as Earl answers the phone.

Peter Wakowski, self-titled "P-Dub", is the nation's tenth ranked player according to ESPN. If you don't know by his nickname, he's a swagged-out white boy that resembles Channing Tatum. He stands at six-feet-seven-inches and weighs two hundred pounds, and the boy can shoot the leather off the ball. Like Big Earl, Peter and Sir go way back from competing against one another in the AAU circuits and basketball camps.

"Preacher Man!" Peter says jubilantly. "I called Sir and got his deacon instead. Today must be my lucky day."

"Don't play with the Lord," Earl says in a stern but loose tone. "Nah, I'm just messing with you," he smirks, turning the phone toward Rick and Sir who are still in mid laugh.

"What up Pete!" Sir shouts.

"Hi Peter," Rick says in a flat mocking tone.

"What up, Sir! Hello, Ricky," Pete mocks back. "What's taking y'all so long to get here? We're gonna be on lockdown real soon. I'm trying to go to the girls' team hotel before the dog and pony show starts. They got a few of them on that baller babes IG page. I'm trying to see what it's looking like in person. You feel me? Can't be out here getting catfished."

"What makes you think they want you, fool?" Sir says chuckling.

"Come on now, two words. 'P. DUB'. Now just get here or get left behind. I'm out."

"We'll see you in a few." Earl hangs up the phone and shakes his head. "He'll never change."

"NEVER!" Rick and Sir says in unison.

The driver continues to maneuver through the bumper-to-bumper Atlanta afternoon traffic as Earl, Rick and Sir share stories about this past season, the ups and downs of the grind, and the long drawn out recruiting process. Big Earl was still undecided on his school of choice as well. From the third-row seat, Rick leans forward, in between the two.

"So, what's up Big Earl! When you gonna sign your letter of intent to Duke? It'll be cool to have the state champions of Illinois and Texas holding it down in Durham." Rick puts his arm around Sir's shoulder, making sure to flash his first of two state championship rings.

"You know the good Lord wouldn't allow me to wear a Blue DEVIL'S uniform. Besides, I hear Sir might sign with UNC. Me and point guards get along *really* well. Shooting guards, *ehhh…* But I'll be praying for you though." Earl smiles, cutting his eyes at Sir.

"Nah, big fella." Rick responds. "You got it all wrong. We're not battling all season like we did in high school. We're cornering the NCAA. Sir is going to the PAC-12 or SEC, while I hold down the ACC."

"Since when did you become Sir's spokesperson? Let my man speak for himself." Rick and Earl look at Sir in unison, curiously awaiting a response.

"Fellas, I'll be dealing with this all weekend, come-on now… But I will let y'all in on a little secret." Sir replies. There's a pause. Rick and Earl get more anxious. The driver is even eyeing through his rearview trying to get the scoop at this point.

"If I had to choose today..." Sir says with a sigh. "I'd have to choose… The Big 3: Me AND BOTH Y'ALL's SISTERS!"

Rick jokingly throws Sir in the headlock as the entire car bursts out laughing and the car pulls in front of the hotel.

"Will you guys relax?" Sir says laughing it off. "I don't know yet. I'm still figuring things out. Let me enjoy these few days man. Please?"

"Alright, alright." Earl says, opening the door.

"Thank you. Now, let's do it. Rick, you're already committed, so you can stay in the car." Sir says, closing the door in Rick's face.

From inside the SUV, Rick shouts. "Oh, that's cold. Duke fans are everywhere. Open the door big fella, my fans are waiting." The boys are met by a flurry of autograph requests and questions about college. The festivities of the weekend are just getting started.

"Rule number one, don't touch my braids," the tall athletic young lady says with a half-smile. She's wearing a black t-shirt with the words 'Do Not Disturb' across the chest, some ripped denims and trendy kicks. "I don't know what they do where you're from, but touching a black woman's hair is a cardinal sin, you hear me?"

"My bad," Peter says, catching himself. "P-Dub never saw them so small. No disrespect, beautiful, I was just curious." He looks around at the mostly empty lobby. Just a few media people, coaches and personnel for the all-star game are chatting. "This is a nice hotel, much calmer than ours. I never got your name."

"P-Dub, right?" The young lady replies as she stops scrolling through her phone. "I thought your name was Peter, according to your IG page." Peter shoots a surprised look her way. "Yeah, I know who you are, Mr. Oregon," she continues. "And this is how it works on our side. All the bright lights and fans, we don't get that often. Oh, the name is Ryan."

"Ryan Williams," Peter interrupted. "First Team All-State in New York, committed to the University of Connecticut. I know who you are too."

"Now that we know we are aware of who we are, say 'hello' and introduce yourself before you start touching my braids," Ryan says, with a smirk. "And they're supposed to be small. They are called microbraids for a reason."

"Ohhh, micro... braids. P-Dub is learning. I got you."

"You're much shorter in person. I almost didn't notice you." She says as two other young ladies approach them, each dressed for a day out on the town.

"I see, you got jokes. But where are you all headed?" Peter asks as he scans the ladies from head to toe. "Ladies, I'm P-Dub. Excuse Ryan for being rude and not introducing us."

"Girls, meet Peter." Ryan says. "He's from Oregon and has a hitch in his shot, but I guess he's ok." The ladies all break out laughing. "We're going over to the AUC to hang out."

"What's the AUC?"

"The Atlanta University Center," Ryan replies. "a connecting spot for Morehouse, Spellman, and Clark. My cousin goes to Spellman, so we're going to hang out."

"Oh, word?" Peter says enthused. "I'm in!"

Ryan gives Peter a look up and down, looks at the other young ladies, glances back at Peter while shaking her head and says, "Nah, I don't think so. We're trying to keep a low profile and you're dressed like a billboard for the Mickey D's game. Every piece of gear they gave us, you have it on."

"Oh, P-Dub can turn his shirt inside out. You won't even know I'm there."

"Hmmmm, I don't know. What y'all think?" Ryan says, glancing at her teammates. They both shrug in unison. "Listen, you can go but you have to stop talking in third-person."

Flashing a broad smile, Peter replies, "Bet."

"Ok let's jump on the shuttle before anyone sees us."

A staple during the days surrounding the McDonald's All-American game is the visit to the Ronald McDonald Charities House which houses around fifty families with sick children. The purpose is to keep families and children together with around-the-clock access to resources necessary for their survival. The boys' and girls' teams take pictures, sign autographs, color, draw and play games with the kids as they learn about some of their sicknesses. This is a very heartfelt moment for most of the athletes as they realize how fortunate they are to be healthy and doing what they are doing.

Sir sits across from an eight-year-old resident of the house playing checkers. The kid jumps Sir's final piece taking the win, lighting up with excitement.

"Dang, again? What are you, the Steph Curry of checkers?"

"Oh, you ain't know? I'm Steph Curry with the hop, boy." The kid cleverly makes reference to lyrics from a song by Drake.

"I see!" Sir says, laughing, before noticing Rick leaning over toward him in the midst of playing connect four with a little girl.

"Sir, I hate to keep bugging' you with this, bro, but P is on me about the three of us getting together for dinner." Rick says. "I know you have got a lot going on, but, man, you gotta tell me what's up, and I'll know how to move on it."

Every mention of Percy dampens Sir's mood. He no longer wants to deal with Percy, but he doesn't know how to tell him, and he definitely doesn't want to put Rick in the middle of it. It would be easier knowing how to survive without him. "I'll let you know later, bro." Trying to hide the dishonesty on his face, he hears a familiar voice.

"Aye yo, Sir! Catch," yells Peter, before tossing a small rubber hand-sized basketball his way. Sir stretches out to catch the overthrown ball laughing.

"Sheesh! Your passing game is off, bruh." Sir teases.

"That's cause shooters shoot, my boy. No need to be able to pass. But what I do need is for you to sign that there for me," Peter says as he hands him a Sharpie marker.

"What am I signing this for, Pete?"

"For that big booty nurse over there."

"Hey, man," Sir warns, motioning to all the children around them. "Be respectful of the kids."

"My bad. That *nice bodied* nurse. She said her nephew is a huge fan of yours, and I told her I'd get you to sign that ball for her, being that we boys and all."

"And what do you get out of it, Pete?"

"Her number," he grins. Sir rolls his eyes and signs the ball. "I think it's a fair exchange. You know, out of all the college visits I went on, there were no sisters like her on campus. And after yesterday, sisters like that are going to have to be mandatory."

"Aw man, Pete." Sir expressed. "What happened yesterday?"

"Three letters," Peter replies. "A-U-C."

"What's that?"

"The Atlanta University Center." Peter continues. "It's where Morehouse, Spellman and Clark University all connect. I went over with a few of the ladies from the girls' team."

"When did all of this happen?" Sir says confused.

"You all were taking forever to get to the hotel yesterday, so I made a move. It was nothing but bad sisters everywhere, music playing and a bunch of dudes with matching jackets with letters on the front marching around. Not like soldiers but with like a rhythm to it. It was like a non-stop party."

"You mean fraternities, fool?" Sir says laughing.

"Yes!" Peter exclaims. "That's what Ryan said they were called."

"Oh, so now you on a first name basis with Ryan Williams now?" Sir mocks.

"Yeah, whatever. I'm just saying, wherever I end up going for school, it has to have some kind of flavor."

"I hear you Pete, but what about the school's reputation, man?"

"I ain't studyin' all that. You know we ain't gon' be there too long anyway. They keep tryin' to fool me with all these Rachel Dolezal looking breezies. I ain't goin'. I need a chick that grew up on her nana's corn bread and jumped Double Dutch everyday of her childhood."

"And what would you know about any of that growing up in Portland, Oregon, Pete?"

"Everything! You know my mom kept me down at the urban youth community center with her. You've seen my 'Gram. Poppin with sistas. Man, I was at USC, and they tried to impress me by meeting Clint

Eastwood's granddaughter. I don't even like his movies! Now, if they would

have showed me Megan Good's cousin, or any chick named… Shaneka, a

boy would have signed that letter of intent on site."

"Just forget basketball and the school itself huh?"

"Aye, the way I figure, I'm one and done regardless. But in that one

year I am in college, I'm trying to have some real fun. You feel me,"

spinning the ball on his middle finger. He stops the ball's rotation, looks at

Sir's signature and throws him a nod. "Good lookin' out, man. You been

lookin' out for ya boy ever since five-star camp and you still lookin' out for

me now. That's why I *rocks* with you. Now, please excuse me, I'm about to

try to go get my temperature checked or something." Peter says before

walking over to the nurse holding the ball high in the air and pointing. "Miss

lady, did P-Dub deliver for you or what?"

Sitting at the corner of the bar in his plush Atlanta hotel, Percy,

already a few too many drinks in, hangs his head low. Rumblings in the

room consisted mostly of the buzz surrounding the McDonald's All-

American game and the upcoming NCAA Final Four. Percy never thought there would be any doubt during a moment like this. This is the point where all things should be coming together and clicking. In his eyes, he should be silently the king of the room. Unbeknownst to anyone, he would have key chess pieces in the All-American game as well as the future of the NCAA. While his usual calm and confident demeanor is slipping, he knows he has time to salvage the uncertainty of his status with Sir, but the window is closing on him. He isn't the type to falter in situations like this, but ever since he first met Rick and Sir that summer night in Chicago, Sir has always come off as challenging—always willing to resist until he either was convinced, deemed you trustworthy, or forced. That pattern continued during different points throughout their relationship.

One particular time Percy reflects on most is Sir's decision to attend Jordan Prep High School. When it came time to choose a school, the basketball community in Chicago knew that Rick and Sir were Percy's boys. Whether it be a recreational league, AAU, or the school's team, if it was about Rick or Sir being involved, they had to go through Percy. The plan Percy put together was for Rick and Sir to attend separate power schools in different competition classes so they could both be state champions, All-

Americans, and never have to step on each other's toes to take the city over, like they said they envisioned from the first day he met them.

Simeon and Bogan were the best schools in the city in their respective classes, and it was laid out for Sir to go to one and Rick to the other. However, Jordan Prep, the newly built state-of-the-art STEM school in his own neighborhood, intrigued Sir because he wanted to be closer to home. He felt he made a big enough buzz during AAU to solidify his status as a top prospect, despite not attending a powerhouse high school. He thought, if Anthony Davis could do it, then why couldn't he.

Glancing down and reminiscing further, Percy's phone rings. It's Rick. "What's up?" Percy answered.

"What up, P?" Rick says over a noisy background. "It's loud in here. Hope you can hear me. We're leaving the Ronald McDonald House. I can meet up for dinner tomorrow after the three-point shootout and dunk contest. They have us on lockdown any other time."

"Ok cool, and your boy?"

"No cap, you know I'll always keep it real with you, P. Something is going on with Sir. I really can't call it at this point. He told me he'd let me know about dinner, but I wouldn't bank on it. I'll let you know. He ain't sounding right."

"Don't press it. Give him some time. He'll come to his senses. Keep your eyes on him when you can."

"I got you. Hit you later," Rick says as he hangs up.

Percy slams his phone down. The bartender asks, "Are you alright, man?"

Sarcastically, he exclaims, "Yeah, I'm fine. Can't you tell?" Before the bartender could respond, "Just pour me another drink and spare me the counseling session." Complying, the bartender throws his hands up, wanting no smoke with Percy.

Chapter 5 – The Letter

After the conversation at the barbershop, Coach Bradford was on the hunt for as much information about Sir's grandfather, Aldis, as he can find. He goes to Louis Stokes Library checking out old yearbooks, newspaper clippings and all archives the university has. He discovers Aldis was more iconic than he was led to believe. This man wasn't just a hooper. He was a game changer of his time.

Coach Bradford finds that Aldis Walker, nicknamed Sir for the way he held court on the basketball court, not only had a career average of twenty-seven points and seven dimes per game from the years of 1967-1970 for Howard University, but he also marched with Dr. Martin Luther King, Jr. for civil rights, was a member of The Olympic Project for Human Rights (OPHR), and stood tall with the organization as an advocate to boycott the 1968 Olympics. While the boycott failed to materialize in support against racial segregation in the United States and racism in sports in general, Aldis and Lou Alcindor with other Black-American basketball players refused to participate in those Olympics.

What he also uncovers is Aldis was recruited by the University of Kentucky and would've been Adolph Rupp's first African American recruit, but he turned down the offer to instead play for Howard University, a school he felt had his best interest at heart socially, racially, and economically. He wanted to play for a coach that looked like him and could relate to his plight as a black man living in America and playing sports. In a letter he titled, *Slave to the Game,* Aldis explained how those reasons were the determinant factors for his choice to attend and play for Howard over Kentucky.

This is great, insightful news to Coach Bradford! He has to get his hands on that letter. He wonders if Sir knows this about his grandfather, and if he doesn't, he is going to be the one to enlighten. He frantically prints out the information and hurries over to the athletic building, where the letter he hadn't noticed before, resides in the university's trophy case.

Coach Bradford returns to Burr Gymnasium, home of Bison basketball. Instead of going to his office, he heads to the hallway where the trophy case covering the length of the entire wall, displays trophies and photographs of the university's most revered athletes and the athletic program's achievements. He walks down the glass case, peering inside frantically searching for Aldis Walker's name. On a shelf, he sees a folded jersey with the name "*Walker*" across the back. He had walked past this trophy case about a thousand times during his tenure as coach and has looked inside but never had this item caught his attention. But there it was, right next to Aldis' picture and sneakers, the original handwritten letter, *Slave to the Game*, inside a frame. Determined to get a copy of this letter, he heads to the Athletic Director's office to inquire about a way inside the case.

Upon entering the office, Coach Bradford sits in a chair while the receptionist calls the AD from the adjoining office. "Mr. House, you have Coach Bradford here to see you."

Tim House is in his office practicing his swing on an indoor golf putting strip. Adjusting his stance, he calls Coach Bradford inside.

"Afternoon, Corey. Do you play?" he asks, swinging a soft practice golf ball on a tee.

"No, I can't say that I do."

"Golf is a money sport, Corey. Learn to play, and you've got an in. Do you know how many major business deals are held while playing golf?"

"Nah, I'll have to look into it." Corey says while taking a seat. "Tim, there's a letter in the trophy case. You think I can get a copy of it?"

"I don't see why that would be a problem. What is this letter, and why do you need a copy?" he asks before taking another swing.

"Well, there's a really great kid I'm interested in recruiting, and I think it will help."

"Is this a local kid," Tim asks as he places the club back in its carrying case before sitting behind his large wrap-around desk.

"He's from Chicago, but…"

"You know Corey, we're not expecting you to do the exceptional here. I wouldn't waste too much of my time running all over the country recruiting players."

"Well, Tim, actually winning…"

"Listen, don't worry about winning. We're not a basketball school. You just focus on graduating the boys we do get."

"I intend to have a high graduation rate as well as win…"

"Academics, as I've said before, is what brings the money in here. And our alumni love to see our athletes graduate. I'm sure you understand that. Now, if you don't have any other pressing issues, I have to take care of some other pressing business," AD House says, getting up from his desk and leading Coach Bradford out the door.

Later that evening, in his home, Coach Bradford is in the bathroom with his wife, Mia, preparing for bed. "Babe, I discovered so much while researching this kid's grandfather. Then I went to Tim's office to ask him about getting a letter out of the case that I think will help me recruit Sir Walker, and do you know what this man tells me?"

His wife looks at him through the mirror while wrapping her hair.

"This man basically tells me it's okay to lose. I'm not just gonna sit back and lose, Mia. I didn't take this job to sit back and get a check and watch these boys lose. You know that babe. Every time I tried to tell him that being comfortable losing wasn't a part of my makeup, he cut me off."

Mia purses her lips while Coach Bradford is rambling and refusing to let her get a word in edgewise. She takes a bobby pin out of her mouth, puts it in her hair and ties a scarf around it.

"…Talking about this is an academic school. Sports are not the focal point. Just graduate the boys, as if I don't want to do that too. That man makes my blood boil sometimes. No wonder the school hasn't had a winning program since he's been there."

Mia walks over to her husband. She puts her hands on his face and says, "Babe, I think you have great potential. You know you're a great coach." She picks up a face towel and wipes toothpaste from the corner of his mouth. "You can't solve every issue tonight."

"Babe, I damn near just wanna walk away. How am I supposed to win when my own AD ain't even on my side? What do you think? Is it worth it even to try?"

Mia sits on the white marble bathroom counter and pulls her husband to her. "You're exactly where you're supposed to be. You say you refuse to lose. Okay, so refuse to quit."

Coach Bradford takes his wife's face in his hands and kisses her forehead, her cheeks, her nose, and then her lips. "You're right. What would I do without you?"

"You know babe, I ask myself that very same thing. Lord, what would he do without me?" Mia says, smiling and winking at her husband.

The next day, Coach Bradford marches back into the AD's office. As he crosses past the receptionist desk, he looks to see if Tim is around. Noticing he's in the clear, he quietly asks, "Aye, Jannette, do you know how I can…"

Before he could finish, she holds up the key to the trophy case and whispers, "You didn't get this from me," winking and then handing him the key. "Good luck."

Coach Bradford smiles with excitement, mouthing, "Thank you," then darts out the door.

Chapter 6 – #PowerMoves

It's the last few minutes of the McDonald's All-American game, Big Earl sets a screen for Sir. "Right there. Now go!" Sir finds him rolling to the basket and throws the alley-oop. "Get it, big man!"

"Watch out below!"

Big Earl goes up and lands a slam dunk before hopping down and high-fiving Sir.

"These two, look good together. That's the fourth time tonight they've hooked on that play." The commentator boasts.

"It sure is. And with them both still being undecided, I know some coaches would love to package them up." The *other* commentator confirms.

Sir shakes a defender up court, then kicks it back to Peter for three. Peter sinks it from the top of the key.

"And Peter Wakowski can't be too mad at Sir tonight either. That makes his fifth three-pointer, all assisted by the nation's top recruit, *Sir Walker."*

Peter points at Sir back-peddling down the court and Sir points back at him smiling.

"That Sir sure can find them, can't he?"

"He sure can. But don't blink, here he comes again."

Sir explodes up the court, fast breaking by himself. The crowd rumbles in excitement as Sir goes up for a slam dunk. He jogs down the court to chest bump one of his teammates as the buzzer sounds. That's game.

After the game, Sir stands off to the side of the court with a sportscaster, doing a postgame interview.

"Congratulations on the win, Sir, and being this year's McDonald's All-American MVP."

"Thank you. It's truly an honor and a dream come true."

"I can imagine. Of course, college is the next step for you, but the question the world wants to know the answer to is, do you have any idea where that might be?"

Peter comes up from behind, jokingly interjecting, "He's going to Uptown Downtown University with me!"

They all laugh as Peter exits the frame of the camera.

"Yeah, what he said." Sir agrees.

"You two looked really good out there together. With the both of you still being undecided, is there any chance we may see you two in the same uniform next season?"

"I wouldn't mind playing alongside Pete at all. But who knows? We both have really good schools looking at us, and if one of them matches up, you just may. Until then, I'll see you on signing day. Thank you."

"Well, there you have it, sports fans. There is a chance you just may see Sir Walker and Peter Wakowski as teammates next year, but we all have to wait until signing day to find out."

As Sir exits the court, he avoids eye contact with Percy, standing with his arm around Rick, talking in his ear, but looking Sir's way.

As the fellas arrive at Hartsfield-Jackson airport, they dap up and say their good-byes. Big Earl turns to Sir and says, "Don't make no moves without me fam', let me know what you're thinking about doing before you do it."

"Definitely." Sir responds, "I'll hit you up."

Peter chimes in, "Yeah, hit ya' boy up too. If it's something we can make work, let's make it do what it do. You feel me?"

"I feel you."

The three of them depart, going their respective ways, with a sense that something big is about to happen pumping through their mental.

Sir and Joy pull up in front of their home with only the streetlights giving life to their block. As they get out of the Uber, Sir notices Percy's Range Rover parked across the street. The window rolls down just enough so that Percy's piercing eyes are revealed. He looks at Sir and nods, gesturing him over to his vehicle.

Sir takes a deep breath. *Here we go…* "I'll be up in minute," he tells Joy.

"Is everything alright?" Joy asks as she waives at Percy.

"Yeah it's fine, I'll be upstairs soon," Sir replies.

"What's up Percy," Sir dryly says upon entering the Black Ice, strongly scented vehicle.

"You tell me?" Percy responds as he cuts his eyes over at Sir. "You the one not answering my calls, skipping out on dinner in Atlanta, making moves without me."

"I ain't made no moves without you, Percy."

"Oh? Well you have a way of making me feel and think otherwise. Listen, you've been shut down since the State Championship game. I don't know what your deal is, but whatever it is, you need to get it together."

The chess match is in full effect as the two of them sit momentarily in silence, anticipating the other's next move.

Percy sucks his teeth, "Grab that bag from the back seat".

"Percy, man…"

"Percy slightly raises his voice. "Grab the bag!"

Sir reluctantly does so.

"Now open it."

Sir unzips the black designer bookbag, peeling back a few layers of newspaper, uncovering the stacks of money beneath it. Sir gasps at the sight of it.

"That's two-hundred and fifty-thousand dollars. All yours. Enough for you to buy you a car, clothes, nice little chain, watch, whatever... have some money in your pocket and to take care of your momma's bills while you're off at college next year. All you have to do is tell me where we're signing next year, and I can make that bag happen for you and your mother."

Sir stares at the money, wanting to feel the crispness of every single bill but ultimately refusing to touch them.

"You know you wanna touch it. Go on. You'll be the richest eighteen-year-old on campus, for nothing more than what you do best. So, what's it gonna be?"

Sir isn't used to going against Percy. He is the father he never really had—the man who helped make every major decision in life up until this point. His protector, his provider, the man who kept the lights on and the bills paid in Sir's mother's home, making sure Top Ramen and cold winter nights were few and far between. He remembers being twelve and sadly watching his teammates' parents bring snacks and food and drinks in between long days of AAU games while he barely had money to eat one meal, and Percy came and changed all that for him. These are the thoughts racing through his brain as he contemplates answering Percy's question of *What's it gonna be?*

But Sir was hurt. Percy had hurt him. He took the one thing from him that he could never get back, and that changed everything for him. "No matter what school I sign with, this money comes along with it, and you're tied to me and it."

"As fate would have it."

"And there's nothing I can do about it."

Arrogantly, Percy responds, "I don't see why you would want to. Every major program I have made arrangements for you to get the bag. All you have to do is tell me which one you want to go to, cause of course, all of them want you. I will make the phone call, and it's all yours."

Sir covers his face, letting out a deep breath into his hands.

Percy barks at him, "You're not still tripping over that game, are you? Get over it! Get this money and get over it! You know how much money you almost cost me with your emotional bullshit? We don't have time for this, Sir! You understand?"

Sir, filled with emotion and courage, looks over at Percy, responding, "Yeah, I understand. I understand that me and my moms don't need your kind of help anymore. You don't own me. I own me." Placing the bag in Percy's lap, "And you can have the money. I don't need that either." Sir opens the door and exits the vehicle.

Percy yells after him, "Sir… Sir… Get back in the car, Sir. Sir…" Sir never breaks stride and never looks back as he walks toward his home.

Sir walks into his room, flipping on the light. He throws his bag on the floor and plops down on his bed next to a FedEx envelope. He furrows his brow as he looks to see who it is from. To his surprise, it's Coach Bradford reaching out to him yet again. He rips the envelop open. From it, he pulls out a typed letter and xerox copy of Aldis Walker's picture, jersey, shoes and the *Slave to the Game* letter from inside the trophy case. Sir begins to read:

"Dear Sir, this is news to me, and I want to share this with you. The picture is of a display in honor of your late grandfather, Aldis 'Sir' Walker, here inside of Howard's athletic trophy case. I'm sure you already know that he was a standout player here at the university. As I researched him, I found out that he would've been Coach Adolf Rupp's first African-American recruit at Kentucky University alongside a guy named Tom Payne. While Tom chose to accept the scholarship, your grandfather refused to play for a school he thought would think of him as just another black athlete instead of the man he was. While times have changed for Kentucky, unlike many black players at that time, your grandfather had a choice, and he chose Howard University. He wrote about why he made his choice in a letter he titled *Slave to the Game* which still remains in our trophy case. If you haven't read it, I encourage you to one day come read it for yourself. While I would love to have you come play for me and lead this program like your grandfather once did, I know you must choose what's best for Sir. Good luck in choosing where you'll play next year. Best regards, Coach Corey Bradford."

After reading Coach Bradford's letter, Sir takes a moment, hearing Booney's profound words, "*You either change the game, or become a slave to it."* This resonates louder than it did before, and at this moment, Sir knew what he must do.

He quickly grabs his phone, sending a text to Rick: "Still signing with Duke in a few days?"

Rick responds, "Yep! And I hope you sign with somebody we play so I can bust that ass next year. #StateChampion," followed by a "trophy emoji."

Sir texts back, "You wish," followed by a "Hamburger emoji" and the letters "MVP".

Rick replies with a "Side-eye emoji".

Sir laughs at Rick's response as he thinks to hit up Big Earl. But before he can, a text from Earl, with Peter added in the thread, comes through, "So, what we doing fellas? Pop's trippin' and my options are limited! He's really loving the home state team, Texas A&M, and their Christian coach."

Peter chimes in, "Texas A&M? The SEC is full of teams way more promising than them."

"Told you my pops is trippin'."

"Well, I just got off the phone with UCLA and they're talking really good to PAC-12 following white kid like myself."

Sir shoots a baffling response, "You know ain't no sistas hardly there neither, right?"

"Yeah but I did see a lot of good-looking curly head mixed chicks there and I'm not opposed to silicon bodies neither."

"Well, I looked up Howard University and they have a ten-to-one, woman-to-man ratio."

Both Peter and Earl text back, "HOWARD?!!?"

"Did you say ten-to-one?" Peter asks.

Sir laughs, "Yup. All sistas. I'll call y'all in a few. #PowerMove."

Sir grabs Coach Bradford's card from his dresser, dialing his number. The phone rings several times before he picks up.

"Coach Bradford, speaking…"

"Hey Coach, it's Sir Walker. I was wondering how many scholarships you got available…"

Chapter 7 – Family Talk

Earl and his father, Pastor Singleton, are alone in the back of the sanctuary. The polish on all of the woodgrain in the church left a citrusy scent in the air. There is a long creaking noise as Pastor Singleton sighs and leans back against the pew. It's silent enough to hear the choir rehearsing in the next room.

"Howard, you say?" He says.

"Yes sir," Earl replies.

"Courageous," Pastor Singleton continues. "Reminds me of when I decided to go to seminary school instead of going to work after college. Your grandfather wanted me to come back home, help out in the church, and take his seat when the time came."

"So, what happened?"

"Well, while in college, I found that it was a community right here that needed me more than the church back home," Pastor Singleton replies. "I felt it was my calling the Lord placed on my life. The purpose behind it was bigger than me and my family. So, you think this is that moment in your life?"

"Yes," Earl responds.

"Your mother and I are proud of you. What you and your friends are doing by going to Howard is going to be monumental. I have no doubts that it's going to bring the devil out in the process. But the Lord will not take you through anything that you can't handle, if it's his plan for you. We're going to pray and let God lead the way."

Earl places his hand firmly on his father's. "I can't believe I'm about to do this," he says. "But I believe it's what we're supposed to do. We're going to change the game. I love you, Dad. Thanks for believing in me."

"I love you too, son," Pastor Singleton says. "Let's pray. Father God…"

It's silent in the Wakowski household. Peter and his parents are at the dinner table in their modernly designed dining room. The flat screen TV mounted on the wall is on mute. Mr. Wakowski is staring at the top row of the wood grain bookshelf which holds Peter's Oregon Mr. Basketball trophy, Mrs. Wakowski's Community Service plaque, and a Phil Knight bust that Mr. Wakowski received when he retired after twenty-five years in business development with Nike. Music is blaring from Peter's headphones as he moves the food around his plate.

"Take the headphones off at the dinner table," Mr. Wakowski says. "You need to understand what you're getting yourself into. Your mother and I usually allow you to make your own decisions as long as your choices are thought through and reasoned. We don't think that's the case right now."

"We?" Mrs. Wakowski interjects.

"Yes, we," Mr. Wakowski quickly replies.

"Sir and Big Earl are my boys," Peter pleads. "Whether I go to Howard, Oregon, UCLA or anywhere else, I'm only going to experience it for a year."

"You hear your son right now?" Mr. Wakowski says. "He's only experiencing it for a year. Not only does he want to run off to Howard University without our input, but he's also dropping out after a year to go to the NBA. Why spend our money on private school for him to drop out of college after a year?"

"Sweetie listen..." Mrs. Wakowski gathers her thoughts. "I'm not against Howard. The school has a rich tradition, and they have a lot of notable alumni. But have you done your homework? What about the coach? What do you know about him? Is it a good fit? Coach from OU came to the house five times before you started to buy into the program. I think the decision came out of the blue and is rushed."

"Thank you!" Mr. Wakowski says relieved. "See son, listen to your mother. You're talking this, one year and go to the NBA stuff. How many guys have ever done that from an HBC school?"

"HBCU, dad... HBCU."

"Whatever," Mr. Wakowski snaps back, glancing at the TV as a headline goes across the screen: '*NFL COMMISSIONER ROGER GOODELL IS INITIATING A NEW POLICY FOR ON-FIELD PROTESTS BEGINNING NEXT SEASON.*' "You see this crap," Mr. Wakowski says, gesturing toward the TV. "Why bring protests into sports and cause all this scrutiny? You can be demonstrative without being disruptive, and you can still get the results."

"Mom. Dad. I did my homework on Howard and on Coach Bradford," Peter explains. "I have had a bunch of conversations with Coach, Sir and Big Earl."

"PETE…" Mr. Wakowski exclaims.

"Dad, hear me out… Mom, you have spent more time working at that group home than you do here and have had me with you the entire time, and you didn't have to do it. You did it because giving back is your purpose, and in the process, I got a little swag, but I also care about my purpose."

Sensing continued frustration, Mrs. Wakowski looks at her husband while mouthing to let their son finish speaking.

"Dad, where do you think I get the urge and desire to dream big?" Peter reasons. "You tell me all the time how you had to stay motivated and think big to go over to Nike and have the success you had. Am I guaranteed to go to the NBA after one year? No. But if that is what the best players are doing, and I feel like I'm one of the best, then I have to have the same mindset. I want to go to the highest level, and I want to make history. Do something bigger than me. Me, Sir and Earl can go to Howard and make history!"

Mr. Wakowski takes a couple of deep breaths, grabs the remote and turns off the TV. Staring at Peter as he stands up from the table, "I guess you have everything figured out," he says. "But I'll tell you this, there is always two sides to history. Make sure you end up on the right side. Talk some sense into this kid. I'm going out for a drink."

"Mom..."

"Honey let him go," Mrs. Wakowski says to Peter as the door slams. "You have to understand the skepticism that comes with what you're doing. You, Earl and Sir are doing something commendable, but I want you to think about all that comes with it. If you do, and you still feel the same about the decision, you have my support. And for the record, I'm proud of you."

"Thanks, Mom." Peter says, knowing his parents are indifferent about his choice. He knows they don't quite understand what a white kid can actually be gaining from experiencing an all-Black university. Mr. and Mrs. Wakowski were born and raised in Portland, Oregon, and though they are not racist by any means, they never thought their son would take to Black culture as he has. But with Hip-Hop being heavily influenced in his life, by way of basketball, a predominately Black sport, and hours spent with his mom volunteering at the community center, it's really no surprise why he is the way he is. But in the end, like any good parents, they just want the best for their son.

It's 10a.m. on a Friday morning, and the sun is shining unusually bright for a pre-spring Chicago day. Inside Jordan Prep, the gymnasium is packed to capacity like it normally is for the boys' varsity basketball games. Only, no balls are being bounced, and no layups are being shot. The floor is filled with students and fans of Sir's, news reporters from every major news and sports networks, local bloggers, and school staff. Booney stands in the back of the gym behind the throng of cameras, microphones and bright lights, waiting for the arrival of Sir, along with everybody else.

Sitting at the far end of the gym, a stage is assembled directly under the raised basketball goal and the conference and city champion banners Sir help win over the years. In the center of the stage, there's a table with three folding chairs behind it. And on top of the table, four snap-back hats belonging to UNC, Kentucky, DePaul, and Michigan State sit in front of a lone microphone. In a modern era where kids are announcing their colleges of choice via video in a very cinematic way, Sir being the traditional guy that he is, has chosen to do his signing day in a way that fits his personality.

As the crowd continues to talk amongst one another—reporting where they think he might go—after an hour of waiting, the doors open, and Sir and his mother, Joy, finally walk in. A round of applause ensues, welcoming the nation's top recruit. Sir is all smiles as he humbly nods and shakes the hands of those who have come to support his special day. Hand in hand, Sir helps Joy to her seat to the left of his, while Coach Griff, his high school coach, sits to Sir's right. Dressed in a dark blue suit from Macy's with a tie to adorn his crisp white shirt, Sir takes his seat, emulating the postgame press conferences of the pro athletes he hopes to one day become.

Sir taps on the microphone, *Pff, Pff, Pff,* silencing the murmuring among the crowd. "Is this thing on?" he asks, making sure the crowd can hear him. "I want to thank all of you for coming out today. This is a special moment in my life, and it's been tough reaching the decision that I'm about to share with you. First and foremost, I'd like to thank all the coaches who have put the efforts in to recruit me as well as the schools that have showed me the utmost hospitality on my visits. I'd like to thank my coach, my teammates and all the fans who have supported me so far. And to my mom, who's sacrificed so much to get me to this point, I love you. What I'm about to say is about to shock all of you, and it's unfortunate that I don't get to put on the hat of the school that I'm signing with. But after careful consideration, I've decided that next year I'll be playing for Coach Corey Bradford and the Bison of Howard University. Thank you."

Gasps fill the room as reporters fight to get their questions answered. "Sir… Sir… Sir…"

Sir points to a reporter, "You, in the plaid tie."

"Sir, George Wrighster, Unafraid Show dot com. No All-American has ever chosen to play at an HBCU, let alone, the number one recruit. What made you choose to do so?"

"Besides Coach Bradford being a great guy and making me believe that I can grow as a player in his program, I want to do the unthinkable with my career, follow in my grandfather's footsteps and help elevate a program that has the potential to be rich in tradition, just like the existing high-major programs."

"You're a potential 'one and done.' How do you expect that to happen in the one year you're there?" Another reporter asks.

"I mean, I hope to be as successful in achieving what I'm setting out to do in whatever time I spend there, and hopefully it's the start of something big."

More murmuring erupts as reporters begin reacting to the alerts coming through on their phones.

"Sir, are you aware that Earl Singleton and Peter Wakowski just announced that they, too, are attending Howard University?"

With a smile as bright as the sun, Sir responds, "Absolutely. We wanted to do what the Fab-Five did for Michigan but in our own way, and Howard is where we see ourselves best making our mark in the history books."

"Sir… Sir… Sir…" Reporters continue to scream out to get answers, but Sir is over it.

"That's it for the questions for today. I have to get ready to fly out and meet with my new coach. I'll see you all at Howard. Thank you."

Sir rises from his seat, winking at Booney, who points back ecstatically, smiling from ear to ear. Reporters jam microphones in Sir's face as he and Joy exit, limiting his answers as he quickly tries to leave.

" *Yes, you've heard correctly, sports world. Not one, not two, but three of the nation's top ten high school basketball players have all committed to signing with Coach Corey Bradford and the Howard University Bison. It's unprecedented. It's monumental. It's absolutely game changing at its finest,*" an ESPN sportscaster reports.

And that was one of thousands of reports all in awe about what the world is now calling "The HBC-3". In just a few days, it has become a moniker that now adorns the front of t-shirts, hats and hoodies across America. The HBC-3 has become a cultural statement before they've even played one game. What has been discussed, for decades, within the walls of urban barbershops throughout the nation is now a reality—All-Americans choosing to play at an HBCU. And those who are part of the movement are loving every bit of it.

Chapter 8 – Chocolate City

It's late August in D.C., so the weather is just right for the students at Howard. They still have about a week or two to rock their shorts, sundresses, halter-tops and jerseys and show off their oily melanin-rich legs and lean-cut muscles. The HBC-3 have been on Howard's campus for a few weeks now. Today is the first day of class, and they haven't seen it like this—with the hustle and bustle in full effect from students going to and from class, financial aid offices, practices and back to their dorm rooms for mid-day naps. There are also those who have no worries in the world. Some of the students are chilling in the grass or on tables, listening to music, reminiscing about their summer endeavors, and laughing and enjoying being young and black. Then, there is the band playing music to welcome the student body. The majorettes, dressed in their skimpy, shining uniforms, routinely pop their backs to the rhythm and beat, as the members of fraternities and sororities chant and stomp the yard, enticing those who'd love to be a part of such traditions to join.

This is all fairly new to Sir, Big Earl and Peter, strolling through campus taking it all in. All of the beautiful Black women accented by the scent of cocoa butter is especially attractive to Peter who had only hoped and imagined it would be like this, especially after seeing a glimpse of it in Atlanta a few months prior.

"Thank you, God," Peter subtly says, looking up to the heavens after he watches a pair dark female legs, followed by a friendly bright smile, strut by. "I'm in heaven. How come nobody ever told me about this HBCU situation before? I would've committed to coming here years ago!"

"Bruh, I knew what an HBCU was, but man I had no idea it was like this," Sir says, waving at a group of females, crossing past. "Now I know why they call D.C. Chocolate City!"

"Amen to that!" Earl exclaims.

"And a hallelujah, too!" Peter shouts, raising his hands.

With all of the press surrounding the HBC-3, Coach Bradford figures they'll be doing a lot of interviews, so he makes sure the boys are enrolled in a speech class, to make them more than prepared to answer all the questions that would come their way. For Sir and Peter, talking in front of people comes easy, so this class is going to be a breeze. But for Big Earl, speaking publicly is not something he looks forward to. In fact, playing basketball is the only thing he has ever felt comfortable doing in front of a crowd. You would think being a pastor's son and growing up in church where kids had to do speeches for Easter and Christmas, he would be a natural. But not Earl. Speaking publicly terrifies him, and he refuses to do it. On signing day, he didn't make a video or sit in front of a gym and make an announcement like Sir. Instead, he had his father stand before the church and press and tell the people of his son's decision, while he sat behind his dad. So, doing interviews is not in his plan, and he does not like the idea of being in this class.

As the professor goes over the syllabus for the semester, Earl stresses his concerns, whispering to Sir, "Did he just say oral presentation?"

"Yeah. It won't be that bad…"

"Easy for you to say. I'm not getting up in front of this class and presenting nothing."

"Mr. Singleton," Professor Mayhorn calls out.

"Yes, sir?"

"You'll soon have your chance to hold court in my class, but right now is not the time. Please allow me to finish, would you?"

"I'm sorry, Professor. Please continue, sir."

With prayer hands formed, the professor nods his head in gratitude, continuing.

Earl leans over to Sir one more time to say, "I've got to get out of here."

And that's when it happens. At five-foot-seven, caramel-colored skin and silky black hair, she gracefully strolls into the classroom looking like ice cream on a hot summer's day. She hands a pair of keys to the professor, lights up the room with her smile, then leaves. Sir is smitten immediately, and the class can't end fast enough so that he can have the chance to catch up with her and formally introduce himself.

No sooner than the professor says, "All right class…" Sir is bolting out of the door. Exiting the building, looking left and right, he scans the throng of students. Finally, he spots her coral blouse from afar. The race is on, as he sprints in her direction, weaving through students, spinning off a few—ball players will be ball players—and finally catching up with her. Only a few steps away, he quickly tries to gain his composure before approaching. As he does, she turns around noticing that he's slightly out of breath.

"Do you need some water?" she says.

Caught off guard, he responds, "Oh, nah I'm cool." Knowing he does. "Damn, you walk fast."

"Oh, you were trying to catch up with me?"

"Absolutely. I wanted to introduce myself." Extending his hand, "Hi, I'm…"

"Sir Walker. I know exactly who you are."

He smiles. "Well… That's cool. And you are?"

"Alexandra Myles. My friends call me Alex." Shaking Sir's hand.

"And what does your boyfriend call you?" He cleverly pries, "Beautiful, I hope?"

Alex laughs, "That was cute. Nice little way to compliment me while investigating if I'm in a relationship. Two points for you. It was nice meeting you, Sir. Enjoy your day." She smiles, walking away.

Baffled, Sir scrunches his face then gives chase once again. "That's it? You're just going to walk away?"

"Yes, I have to get to my class."

"But you never answered my question?"

"I gave you my name, didn't I? Maybe the next conversation, I'll give you more."

Stumped, Sir stops walking, then he smiles as the thought of a second conversation hits him. "So that means we're gonna talk again?" He yells out.

Alex turns and smiles and continues walking.

Sir confidently turns in the opposite direction. Peter and Earl approach, having seen the tail end of Sir's conversation.

"She dissed you, huh?" Peter interrogates. "You should've asked your boy how to get at that. I would've totally put you on game."

Sir cuts his eyes and twists up his lips at Peter, as to say, *Man, please.*

"What? I would've."

As the three of them file off, Sir can't help but to think about Alex's radiant smile and the opportunity to really get to know her. In high school, under the helm of Percy, there were not many opportunities to really get to entertain a *chick*. He had some fun here and there, but never seriously dated anyone. For Percy, it was all about basketball and nothing else. Now, Sir could sense the difference in his newfound freedom already. And he was eager to embrace it in every way possible.

Chapter 9 – Things Done Changed

It's the first day of practice and the Howard men's basketball team is gathered in their locker room at Burr Gymnasium. It's far from being state-of-the-art, yet, it has a very modern, intimate feel. The fellas are sitting around undressing, hyped about getting on the court today and clowning around as a band of brothers usually do, talking about each other and blasting J. Cole's music through one of the player's Beat Pills. This is a universal vibe across the country for basketball teams getting ready to take the practice court.

Coach Bradford enters with his coaching staff and team mangers carrying oversized boxes filled with Nike apparel. When the HBC-3 made their announcements to sign with Howard, Nike rolled out the red carpet for Coach Bradford and the Bison, signing him to a very lucrative, impromptu, two-year, two-hundred-thousand-dollar annual endorsement deal, giving the school a four-year, eight-million-dollar apparel deal, as well as, assigning one of Nike's strength and conditioning trainers to work with the team, proving just how much these three kids are worth. However, it doesn't even compare to the tens of millions that are about to be made this year alone.

In addition to the new apparel deal, the school signed an eight-game national TV deal, a first in school history. And because Burr Gymnasium only seats twenty-seven hundred, the home games have been moved to the NBA arena in downtown D.C. where at least twenty thousand spectators can file in to watch the must-see HBC-3. It's amazing what three eighteen-year-old athletes have changed by signing their names, and yet this is the tip of the iceberg.

As the team managers crack open the boxes and pull out the two newly designed game-day uniforms, the guys marvel at what they'll soon be wearing a few months from now. Not everybody is happy about the arrival of the HBC-3 and the forthcoming changes, in particular, Eric Sanders, a senior on the team and the returning starting two-guard from last year's dismal season. This was supposed to be his year to shine, but he knows with the arrival of Sir, Peter, and Big Earl, he'll be forced to take a back seat.

"Damn, Coach! This is what life is like when we get a few All-Americans on the squad, huh? We get that fly shit. That Oregon Duck shit!" He patronizingly comments.

The team all laugh, poking fun at the HBC-3.

For the HBC-3, cameras and reporters had become a part of their lives. Popularity was nothing new to them. They had been in the limelight since, damn near, freshmen year of high school. At this point, they act like the cameras are not around and only speak to reporters when they deem it necessary. Of course, excluding Big Earl, who does not respond much at all, except for, "No interviews for me. Be blessed," as he keeps it pushing. But for the rest of the team and coaching staff, this is all new territory. They have never had reporters and cameras in the gym watching them practice and paying so much attention to their every move. This is only something they'd seen the big boys go through. They couldn't have imagined this type of attention at Howard University. Everyone on the team has become instant pieces to this blooming story.

Every time a player is not involved on the court, a microphone is shoved in his face, asking him questions concerning his new teammates—the how's and why's and what's it like, etc. They have suddenly become a part of a reality show that they didn't sign up for. The more attention they get, the more they embrace it. Their Instagram followers begin to grow and likes on pictures begin to come in by the thousand. Having the HBC-3 as teammates is a win-win for everybody, popularity wise. With all this attention every day, Coach Bradford is forced to step up his game. Though he had never coached this caliber of players before, he does not want to look like he has no clue what he is doing, so he runs as many plays for the HBC-3 as he can, and when all else fails, it's the Sir show. It looks good for the cameras, at least in practice. But the more Coach Bradford's favoritism grows, so does the resentment. A balance needs to be found and found fast.

One day in practice, the team is spread out, shooting free-throws on the six basketball goals throughout the gym—two to three players per basket. Deciding which teammates paired up with whom is the choice of the players. Naturally, Sir is typically paired with Big Earl and Pete, but he does switch up his groups, using the time for bonding with other teammates. By this time, the team has been practicing for a few weeks, but because there is a bit of tension between Sir and Eric, the two of them have never chosen to be in the same group.

Prior to this day, Coach Bradford called the two of them into his office, hoping to reconcile their differences. In the meeting, Eric complained that favoritism was being shown, and Coach Bradford stressed that he would attempt to do better. The reality is Sir is the better basketball player, and Coach Bradford is caught up in the HBC-3 hype just as much as the rest of the country.

In an attempt to smooth things over, Sir decides to shoot his free-throws today with Eric and Thomas "Big Tommy" Walson, a talented six-nine big man from Virginia who, too, is a senior. Big Tommy thinks of the HBC-3 as his little brothers and is more than happy to play alongside them. Though he feels the favoritism also, he has chalked it up to *it is what it is* and is in it for the ride. As the three of them are shooting, not many words exchange between Sir and Eric. Tommy is saying things to the both of them as they rotate along the free-throw line to get them to engage in conversation. Eric is not having it. Even Sir attempts to say things to him, like complimenting his form, but the more they try, the angrier Eric grows.

"So, tell me this, freshy," Eric condescendingly remarks. "What was that bag like for you and the others to get y'all to come here? Two-fifty? Five-hundred?" He shoots a shot.

Big Tommy squints his eyes at Eric like " *Dude, WTF?!* " then quickly turns to Sir to watch his response.

Sir grabs the rebound and laughs to himself before passing the ball back. "Wasn't no bag, bruh. We just came here on our own."

"Is that right? All that money you been taking throughout your high school career and you just decided to come here for free? That's what you want us to believe?" He shoots.

"Free country, bruh. You can believe what you want."

"Well me and some of the guys believe you threw your state championship game, and we were wondering how many games you plan on throwing while you're here?"

This gets to Sir, gripping the ball, approaching Eric quickly. "What'd you say?"

"You heard me," Eric barks, approaching Sir back.

Big Tommy steps in between the two, "Aye, come on guys!"

"Nah, let the young tadpole get his frog legs."

"Fellas…" Tommy says, looking around referencing that they be mindful of the eyes and cameras around.

Sir grits his teeth, calming himself. "It's cool. I'm done practicing for the day. I'll see y'all later." Sir says, storming off to save face.

"That's cold." Tommy says to Eric.

"He's a cheater, my guy. It's only a matter of time before he's exposed."

Chapter 10 – Smiling Faces

op up out the beddd, turn my swag onnn…" Peter sings along with the *Soldier Boy* track blasting throughout their dorm room. "That's my joint, bro!" He says while checking in the mirror to make sure his gear is right. "It speaks to my soul!"

"Every hip-hop song speaks to your soul, bruh." Sir shouts, standing in boxers, ironing his clothes.

"Bruh… Bruh…" Peter plays with the word. "I like how you say that. And you're right. Something about a hot sixteen that just does wonders to my spirit. If I wasn't a hooper, I'd definitely try my hand in rap."

"Why don't you *UNWRAP* this box, so we can see what kind of snacks your mom done sent us."

"Go on and crack it open, bruh."

"Don't mind if I do," Sir says, rubbing his hands together.

Peter's mom sends him care packages, full of the essentials she thinks he needs along with chips, cookies, candy, and other snacks to cater to his sweet tooth. This kind of gesture was unheard of for Sir, but he surely appreciates Mrs. Wakowski showing the love. Since she knows the two of them and Earl room together, she always puts enough in there for the three of them.

As Sir dives in into the box of goodies, he shouts, "If I didn't need the energy of this party, I'd stay right here and run through all of this!"

Peter flops down on the couch, next to Sir. "Oh, we're going to this party! I look forward to these parties. Don't you dare try to deprive me… and you, of all the beautiful sistas who want to put their sweaty bodies all over ours."

"You don't need me."

"Yes, I do! I always need you. We're a team, remember? Now get dressed."

Sir twists up his lips at Peter. There's a knock at the door, followed by the entrance of Big Tommy.

"What's up fellas!" Tommy's deep voice projects.

"Tommy!" Sir, shouts.

"Tommy! What's up, bruh!" Peter hollers.

"Oh, you an Alpha, now?" Tommy asks.

Peter is stumped. "Come again?"

"Yeah, Pete," Sir chimes in. "Remember your trip to the AUC? The guys with the letters on the front of their shirts?"

"Oh, the fraternities!" Peter replies.

"Yup, the Alphas," Tommy says, "the one's that dress in the black and gold that be stomping the yard and the parties doing this…" Tommy claps his hands and stomps his feet. "The Bruhs is their nickname."

"Oh, word! I like those dudes," Peter exclaims.

"Yeah man," Tommy explains. "Alpha Phi Alpha Incorporated is one of many black fraternities found on our campus and other HBCUs throughout the country. They are the first fraternity organized for black men, but since them, four other fraternities and four sororities originated. They're known as the Devine Nine and they are part of what HBCUs are built on and stand for."

"I never knew it was that deep my dude," Peter says after hanging on to every one of Tommy's words.

"Indeed," Tommy continues. "Now, while they do community service projects and create networks and all that, they are also the ones that throw the dopest parties on campus. They're throwing the one tonight and I came to see if y'all are going?

"Yeah, we're going. Well… according to Pete, I kind of have to."

"Sweet! It's about to be lit!"

Earl enters the living quarters, dressed in his Sunday's best, looking like someone's daddy. "Y'all almost ready?"

The guys take a look at him and bust out in laughter.

"What's so funny?" He asks.

"We're going to a party, Big Earl, not a baptismal," Sir jokes.

"Yeah, you ain't gonna get no action, dressed like T.D. Jakes," Peter chimes in.

"What? I like T.D. Jakes!"

Both Sir and Peter, exclaim, "We can tell," then laugh.

"We let you live the other times, but this… this is overdoing it! You can't wear no suit to a college party, my dude," Sir says.

"Yeah, bruh," Peter, agrees. "Big Tommy, tell us you have something in your closet you can give our dear deacon brother that's a little less... Sunday revival?" Feeling slightly embarrassed, Earl looks side-eyed at Peter.

Tommy laughs. "Yeah, I'm sure I got something for him. Come with me, big fella."

"Yes, go with him," Sir jokes but is so serious.

As Earl exits with Tommy, Peter turns to Sir and jokes, "Yo, my man look like he about to pass out communion and ask for offering."

"Dead-ass," Sir responds, stuffing his mouth with a cookie.

After a moment, Peter questions, "Say, bruh, what's dead-ass mean?"

Sir laughs, attempting to school his white homeboy. "Facts... Seriously... I agree with you?"

"Oh, gotcha! Damn, just when I be thinking I be up on my lingo, you hit me with something new."

"Don't even trip, my dude," Sir says. "I got you."

Every year, at the beginning of the school year, there's an alumni fundraiser ball for the university and the who's who of who's show up— politicians, major business owners, very successful alum—they all pour in dressed to the nines to talk business, money, politics, and to dance and drink. This night would be no different. While the members of the basketball team are partying with beautiful girls and grinding slowly at some point, Coach Bradford is shaking hands, fake laughing, and for the lack of better words, 'kissing ass'. It comes with the territory. The boosters of the university want to meet and mingle with the staff they're giving their money to and know that it's in good hands. With the HBC-3 now attending the university, Coach Bradford is the man that everyone wants to see.

No sooner than he and his lovely wife, Mia, walk through the door, as Coach Bradford is helping remove her coat, revealing her oiled shoulders and her shapely body though her black shimmering dress, AD House, runs his pompous ass towards them.

"Don't look now, babe, but here comes your best friend," Mia whispers.

AD House approaches, "Corey… Mia… so good to see you! Aren't you looking lovely as can be tonight, Mia?" He leans forward, joking, "There's a lot of money here, Corey had better watch it," causing the first fake laugh of the night to be forced from the two of them.

"Oh, Timothy…" Mia says.

"I hope you don't mind, but I have some very important people that would like to meet your husband. If I could just borrow him for a minute, I promise to have him back before midnight."

Forcing another smile, after yet another bad joke, Mia says, "Sure, go right ahead. I don't think our car will be turning into a pumpkin anytime soon." They all laugh as AD House whisks away Coach Bradford.

Coach Bradford stands at the main bar surrounded by several boosters, sipping their drink of preference, bombarding him with questions about his team and where he sees them going and how happy they are to be fans. Just last year, these same guys barely even looked his way. But now, a new tune is being sung. Among these fine gentlemen, is AD House and Mayor Townsend, D.C.'s middle-aged Black mayor, an avid sports fan, as well as a graduate of Howard who has been a very generous donor.

"You don't know how excited I am about this team," Mayor Townsend exclaims. "And with us having the HBC-3, I don't see why we wouldn't make at least a run at the Sweet Sixteen."

Coach Bradford nods and smiles, "We shall see."

AD House interjects, "Oh Corey is just being modest, Mayor Townsend. I can assure you Coach Bradford here is focused on taking this team as close to the promise land as possible. After all, winning is our top priority here."

Coach Bradford is shocked at the words coming out of AD House's mouth.

"That's what I like to hear," Mayor Townsend exclaims. "Knowing my dollars are going to a potential winning sports program makes me feel good about donating. No offense, but it's hard to get excited about a good English department or stellar Science program. Don't get me wrong, I'm all for academia, but dammit I'm a sports man!" He chuckles. As do the rest of the men.

AD House chimes in, "Aren't we all!"

Coach Bradford can't believe his ears and how fast people change when their best interest is at hand. Makes him wonder if it's even about the kids anymore, or if it has ever been. More importantly, what will happen to him if he doesn't meet their expectations? All these things race through his mind as he tries his best to mask it with yet another disingenuous smile.

Mayor Townsend raises his glass. "Cheers to a run at the Sweet 16!"

On the other side of campus, the Alpha party is in full effect. Sweaty college students are having the time of their lives, dancing and spitting lyrics with no regard for tomorrow. Only thing that matters is right now. The DJ is playing hit after hit and has people feeling good about themselves. It's a good time to be young.

The guys are standing around, taking it all in, enjoying themselves with the rest of the crowd. Sir laughs as he notices Peter's fixation on the fraternities stepping around and through the party, looking like a groupie. He's starting to believe he could be one, as he's stated so, several times this night already. Sir has noticed his growing infatuation for them. Even when Peter was grinding on a female, Sir noticed him peeping the movements of the steppers, envisioning himself in their shoes. Sir too has his eyes on the steppers but for a different reason. He has been watching the Delta sorority all night.

Alex is a member of Delta Sigma Theta Incorporated and has been strolling for most of the party. Since Sir's first encounter with her that day on the yard, they haven't seized an opportunity to have a meaningful conversation. They've caught each other's eyes a few times throughout the night and have shared a smile or two but have yet to engage in conversation. Sir observes an open door after Alex finishes strolling and walks toward the refreshment bar alone. He is not about to let the door close.

The bartender hands Alex her drink. Sir approaches, pulling out a few dollars.

"Let me get that for you," He says, offering to pay.

"You don't have to."

"No, I insist."

"No, really—"

"—My man, how much for the drink?"

"It's free. All drinks are," the bartender says.

"Oh…"

Alex smirks, then walks off. Though slightly embarrassed, Sir still gives chase.

"So, you're a little Delta, huh? Red and white…"

"It's actually crimson and cream. And no, I'm not a little anything. I'm a woman of prestige and honor."

"Oh, my bad. That is a Delta, though, right?"

Alex laughs. She appreciates his efforts. "What can I help you with Mr. Sir Walker?"

"Well, you can start by telling me if you have a boyfriend or not?"

"And if I do?"

"I guess I'll respect it and make like a Delta and step off," he jokes.

"Well, isn't that honorable."

"But I'm hoping you don't," Sir says, wishfully.

"Why, because you're trying to be him?" she asks, having heard the likely response at least a hundred times. But Sir's answer surprises her.

"Possibly," he says. "That's if you're not one of those crazy girls or anything, cause Lord knows I don't need no crazy woman in my life. Stalking me—"

"Boy, ain't nobody trying to stalk you!" She laughs.

"Good!"

The two of them smile at one another. Silence lingers—if there's a such thing as silence at a college party.

He then asks, "Would you like to dance?"

Alex jokes, "Oh I've seen your dance moves and—"

"What? Oh, you were watching me?"

She pauses. "Maybe a little bit," she says, biting her bottom lip.

Her honesty and subtle suggestiveness catch him off guard. Besides her beauty, these little things are what have him smitten. Sir has never been with an older woman before. Alex is two years his senior, so this is all very captivating to him.

As the two of them dance the rest of the night together, laughing a lot, and occasionally gazing in each other's eyes, it is apparent they are very much so, feeling each other.

Chapter 11 – What Team?

*A*s the college basketball season draws near, there has never been more anticipation to see how an HBCU, in particular, Howard University, would do this season against schools like Louisville, Michigan State, and Syracuse. What would normally be 'gimme' games and paid-for wins for these schools, could potentially end up as paid-for losses with Howard University seeing a massive change in the program's roster by landing the top recruiting class in the nation. Since landing the HBC-3, Walker, Singleton and Wakowski, the Bison have seen a huge increase in the school's popularity, endorsements, and ticket sales in which the first four home games have already been moved from the Howard campus to the Capital One Arena to meet the demand. Not to mention, going from no games on national TV to at least 8 scheduled this year as well as a huge payday for second-year, ten and eighteen record-holder Coach Bradford, whose 200k a year salary has been doubled by a 2-year, 400k deal with Nike. But the question on everyone's mind is can Coach Bradford coach the

HBC-3 and the Bison to a winning season, a conference championship and then a solid NCAA run? Because, while we know everything about the HBC-3's abilities, no one really knows anything about Coach Bradford's ability to coach," an ESPN analyst reports.

Sitting in practice, Coach Bradford, looking around at the reporters interviewing his players, he can't help but ponder what the ESPN analyst said about him this morning. It weighs heavy on his mind, and he's never questioned his ability to coach until now. He thought about what Eric said to him about showing favoritism and how he doesn't want to fail anyone but winning is a priority more than ever. He knows the stakes are raised and that he has to be successful. And if he isn't exceptional with the HBC-3 on his team, then he will be who people perceive him to be—a subpar coach who got lucky.

Later that evening, while eating dinner at home with his wife, Coach Bradford sits at the table—a man of few words. Mia can't help but notice her husband's lack of energy.

"Tired, babe?" She asks.

"Nah, I'm okay," he dryly responds.

"Well, you barely said ten words since being home. Something on your mind?"

Coach Bradford closes his eyes, rubbing his forehead with his fingers, thinking about how he's going say what he's about to say. He looks his wife in the eyes and says, "You know, I don't even know." With Mia looking at him, waiting for more, he exhales a deep sigh then elaborates. "I mean, we're a few weeks into practice, things are coming along, the university is receiving lots of attention, but I feel like it's all happening too fast. The Nike deals. The media in practice every day. Every time I look up, a player is doing an interview. The mayor knowing who I am. All because of the presence of these three kids. We haven't even won a game yet, and already we're the Beatles."

"And you're afraid to fail."

"Huh?"

"You're afraid to fail," she repeats. "I know you heard what that sports analyst said about you, and I did too. And he's wrong. You aren't blessed with this opportunity and all the attention because you're incapable of handling it. You are blessed with this opportunity because you are exactly the person who's more than capable of handling it. If you're afraid to fail, then you've already failed. But if you are the man I know you are, then you know it's your failures that have prepared to you to be the great coach that you will be this season." Grabbing his hands from across the table Mia looks into her husband's eyes and continues, "This is your season. Walk into it."

With the muffled sound of the school's band heard playing in the background, dressed in his dark blue game-day suit, Coach Bradford stands in the tunnel of Madison Square Garden, just outside his team's locker room biting his top lip and staring pensively at the cold, cement floor. Reminiscent to the Eminem hit, *Lose Yourself,* his palms are sweaty, and his stomach is turning knots. Only thing missing is vomit and mom's spaghetti, as he tries to drown out today's first-game jitters with thoughts of the encouraging words his wife gave him. "You are a great coach. You are a great coach," he recaps to himself.

"Good luck tonight, Coach," an MSG staff member says, walking by. Looking up and smiling nervously, Corey nods in appreciation.

Today marks a huge day in the school's program. They're ranked in the top twenty-five at the number twenty-five spot in the country for the first time in the school's history. They're playing in the mecca of basketball arenas in front of a sold-out crowd, opening up against the ninth ranked team, and the game is nationally televised as the game of the week. The stage has been set, and Coach Bradford is feeling every bit of the pressure. He knows he needs to relax, so that he can adequately coach his team to victory tonight. And that's exactly what he's in this hallway trying to do.

As he gathers his thoughts, he looks toward the heavens and quotes what his wife often says, "With you God, how can I fail?" Then, he proceeds into the locker room where his coaching staff and players await him.

With all eyes on Coach Bradford, he stands before them, like a commander ready to lead his troops into battle. In true leader fashion, he delivers his speech:

"It's a new day for us. Many of you, and the ones that wore those jerseys before you, sat opposite a team like Syracuse before, not believing you could win. But it's a new day for us. They've prepared. We've prepared. They've got good players. We've got good players. They've got All-Americans. We've got All-Americans. They are ranked, and so are we! It's a new day for us. And they had better be ready, because Howard University is no longer a doormat in college basketball. And with the world watching, we're gonna go out there, get this win in their house, and show everybody that this… is… a new day for us." With a straight face, Coach Bradford looks into the eyes of his players. "Are y'all ready?"

"Yeah," the players say in unison.

"I said, are y'all ready?" Coach Bradford repeats.

"YEAH," the players respond with vigor, jumping to their feet.

"Then let's go out there, show the world who we are, and get this win!"

The Bison run out into the arena; all eyes are on them. The level of excitement is crazy—beyond their imagination. The sea of blue and red Howard paraphernalia is overwhelming in the stands, so much so, one could mistake it for a Howard home game. But it's not, and the home team, Syracuse, is locked and loaded and ready to defend their home court.

Syracuse is returning four starting seniors, two possible lottery picks and coming off of a sweet-sixteen run in the tournament. They're bigger, they're stronger, skilled, and they're far from new to this type of atmosphere. Typically, these two types of programs meet because an elite school like Syracuse pays "ordinary" Howard to come play them, allowing them a regular season warm-up game. They basically pay for a win. Contrary to program status, things read differently and say the two teams are now pretty evenly matched. It'll be up to the Bison to prove the paper and analysts are right.

As the two teams take the court, Sir, walking shoulder to shoulder between Big Earl and Peter, looks at the Syracuse players and says, "Vegas says, they're a six-point favorite, tonight. We'll see about that." As Sir walks ahead of them, Peter and Earl look at each other, confused.

Jump ball! Syracuse gains possession. Immediately, the Syracuse big man gets the ball, plows into Big Earl, then dunks on him. The crowd goes bananas! "Welcome to the big time, Baby Jesus." He taunts. Earl grimaces.

Having his teammates' back, Sir makes sure to get the ball into Earl's hands for their first play down. Earl jab steps, then spins opposite of the Syracuse big man with finesse, shooting a baby hook. *Swish!*

"God sends his love." Big Earl pleasantly responds.

The game moves at a rapid pace, with the two teams going back and forth. Syracuse's coach is hitting Howard with play after play, and Coach Bradford is countering the best way he can, piggybacking on the HBC-3's talents as much as he can. But after a few ill-advised turnovers and fumbles, Sir begins to trust some of his teammates less and less. There's even been several very noticeable times when Sir opts not to pass the ball to anybody else but Earl or Peter. This creates division on the team almost immediately.

Earl and Peter notice Sir's reluctancy to get the others involved, and they only pass to each other. It starts to look like the team has never played together. The more they become divided; the more Syracuse pulls away.

Coach Bradford paces the sideline in disbelief watching his team fall apart out there. Though the Bison manage not to get totally blown out, the final score of 88-79, doesn't tell the real truth.

After the game, the Howard players sit in the locker room, dejected and divided between its stars and role players.

"Sir this! Sir that! I heard Coach say your name so much, I thought we were in the military!" Eric exclaims.

"You looked like you were in the military—stiff as you were playing," Sir shoots back.

"How would you know how I looked? You didn't look to pass to nobody but Earl and the white boy over here!"

Peter defends himself, "Hey, man, leave me out of this."

"Shut up, white boy," Eric barks.

"Don't be mad cause the white boy plays better than you," Sir responds.

"You crazy! Ain't no white boy better than me!"

"Yo, guys! I'm standing right here… I get it, I'm white."

Coach Bradford enters the locker room, with his tie hanging from his slightly unbuttoned shirt. "What's going on in here? What's all the commotion?"

"Why don't you ask Mr. Ball Hog over here," Eric exclaims.

"You just mad cause you suck," Sir retaliates.

"Don't let all this attention go to your head so much that you think I won't whoop that ass!"

"You're lucky to be having any attention at all with your weak ass!"

Sir and Eric come face to face, about to go to blows, the coaching staff steps in, separating the two of them.

Coach Bradford yells, "Y'all cut that out! This is ridiculous! We're one game in, and already you're fighting. You all are a team!"

"Are we?" Eric asks. "Because it seems that ever since you got *them*, you've forgotten about us. I guess this school was perfect for Sir, cause he ain't never cared about a team neither, no way."

The room falls into an awkward silence and Coach Bradford is left speechless, knowing that Eric could be right about him.

Chapter 12 – No Labels

The Monday after the Bison's first game, the sport's media world goes in on the entire team and Coach Bradford stating the obvious about the team's lack of comradery and how the HBC-3 made a mistake choosing to play with talent on their level. When it came to comments about Coach Bradford, the consensus was unanimous that it looked like he didn't have control of his team. Everybody was panicking after one game, as if no team had ever lost their season opener. Unfortunately for the Bison the hype everyone else created began as soon as the seed, the HBC-3, was planted at Howard, and critics were not allowing them time to blossom. The pressure was on before, but it clearly has gone up a level.

Coach Bradford walks into the gymnasium. He stops mid-stride at the baseline and gets lost in a daze—players are lazily engaging in pre-practice activities, reporters are doing interviews, camera men are filming, and Sir, Big Earl, and Pete are shooting around chatting, isolated from it all.

It was a complete circus. Only one game in, and the thoughts of already having failed weighs heavily on Coach Bradford's mind. He is not about to fail his team. Losing them is not an option.

Coach Bradford yells, "Everybody, stop!" With the gym at a halt and all eyes on him, he looks at the members of the media and says, "If you are not a member of this team or coaching staff, I need you to kindly exit the gym, and do not return until we absolutely have to see you come tourney time." Not only does no one budge, but a few chuckles among the media ensues from the idea Coach Bradford thinks he's going to make the tournament. "Now!" he yells, causing the media and bloggers to scurry out the gym like rodents when a room is illuminated.

Now standing with only his staff and players, Coach Bradford says to them, "Take your uniforms off." The players all look around at each other confused.

"What you on, Coach?" Tommy says with his face scrunched up.

"Just take them off. And your shoes too." The players don't budge—still confused.

"Aye, ahh… Coach…" Eric speaks out.

"OFF," Coach Bradford yells again. Slowly, the players begin undressing. "Socks, wristbands, headbands, everything but your compression shorts. Coaches, you too." More confused than the players, the coaches do as their leader says. And he joins them.

As they're undressing, Peter whispers to Sir, "Bruh, this has got to be a black school thing, because I've never done this before."

Just as confused as Peter, Sir responds, "Man, I don't know what this is."

Abs and hairy bellies are revealed as the entire Bison team and coaching staff stand mid court wearing nothing but compression shorts except for one player whose cheeks are out because he decided to wear a jock strap on this day. Earl casually takes a few steps away from him, secretly questioning his choice of outdated undergarment.

Coach looks at his players and staff with a sense of guilt in his heart, and he says, "Here we are, standing stripped of all labels and titles and distractions that said we had to be this, and we had to do that. We are not bound by these things. From this moment forth, no longer will we let them dictate what we are and who we become. We are more than the attention this team has been getting for doing nothing. And I am the number one culprit of letting it go to my head and neglecting what's going to make us special this year, and it's not one or two players or a ranking or a brand across our chest and shoes. It is us, all of us, working together as a unit every day and every night and every time we step on this floor. We all have a part to play, and I'm going to make sure I do my job in involving every one of you so that you can do yours. Yesterday is behind us, and tomorrow is not promised. So, let's make the most out of today and start from here so we all can have one hell of a season."

It's clear to Coach Bradford, by the smirks adorning their faces and head nods, his words have resonated with his players. Sir especially knows, as the best player, what he needs to do.

"Baseline!" Coach Bradford yells out.

Earl raises his hand, "Excuse me, Coach. You think we can dress first?" Gesturing that they're still quite naked.

"Oh, yeah, get back dressed, and then hit the baseline."

As the ball bounces and moves efficiently from one player's hands to the next, for the first time in their early season, the Bison look like a true team. Coach Bradford is very hands-on with all his players, and Sir is distributing the ball and getting all his teammates involved like the true point guard that he is. It's a beautiful day in practice that turns into a beautiful week of practices. No media as Coach Bradford demanded. Just him and his team, learning and bonding with each other.

"As we wind down to end of the first half, the Spartan's are clearly in control of this game." The commentator says to the millions watching the nationally televised game between Howard and twelfth-ranked Michigan State. No sooner than he makes his comment, the shot clock expires on the Bison due to overpassing the ball. *"And there's another turnover for the Bison, making that the eleventh of the half,"* he says in astonishment.

Exasperated, Coach Bradford throws his hands up, "Come on guys, somebody shoot the ball!"

On defense, with seconds remaining in the first half, Sir steals the ball. He has a clear path to the basket. With the crowd on their feet, instead of going up for the score, Sir unexpectedly flips the ball behind him to his trailing teammate. The ball sails out of bounds as the buzzer sounds. The crowd sighs deprived of the highlight they deservingly yearned for.

Sir pats his chest, mouthing, "My bad," to his teammate who looks confused.

Coach Bradford scratches his head in disbelief as he marches toward the locker room with the rest of the team, down eighteen points.

As the teams trail off the court, the commentator reports, *"I'm not sure what's up with these Bison. They seem more out of sync than they did their first game where the HBC-3 took the majority of the shots, but today, no one is taking any shots at all."*

The team enters the locker room with their heads hung low—mostly frustrated and confused about what's occurring on the court. Eric and Sir lock eyes briefly. Eric shakes his head at him before he trails off towards the lockers and Sir towards the direction of the bathroom. Coach Bradford, feeling like his speech and the past week's practice were all for nothing, follows behind Sir.

"What's going on out there, Sir?" he asks, stopping Sir in his tracks. "What, you don't want to play anymore?"

Sir turns around, shrugging his shoulders, "I guess I'm just trying to get everybody involved, Coach. Being the team player the team needs me to be."

Coach Bradford treads these waters with his star player lightly, not wanting to say the wrong thing to worsen the situation. But it's clear Coach doesn't know what to do or what to say. While he's never coached a player of Sir's caliber, he's also never been more confused about how to handle a player either, until now.

"Alright, son. You do that," Coach says, exiting the bathroom.

The start of the second half is much of the same—Sir playing passive aggressively, not taking shots and overly trying to get his teammates involved, so much so, that the defense has started backing off of him. It's not that he's making bad passes, but his teammates are missing shots he could've taken and made, making the outcome worse than it looks. Everyone is baffled by his play. In basketball, all it takes is for one player to carry the load when the others aren't playing well to help keep the team in the fight. Sir has done it time and time before. For some reason, he has chosen not to today. His lack of aggressiveness has become contagious. The turnovers continue to pile up accompanied by missed shot after missed shot. Down twenty-two at the sixteen-minute mark, Coach Bradford uses the media timeout to address his team.

"Do you all not want to play anymore? Is that it?" Coach Bradford aggressively inquires. "Because if that's the case, I'll just sit here and not try to coach, cause you all damn sure are not trying to play." The players look at a Sir for an answer. Eric shoots him daggers, with the thoughts of foul play going through his head. Just like the rest of the world, he knows Sir's capabilities. Seeing him play like this further influences Eric to believe Sir is purposely throwing the game—maybe even for money.

The horn sounds. As the Bison walk back onto the court, Eric approaches Sir. And though he's fuming inside, he elects to take a different approach, hoping to get a positive reaction. "We're not going to ever win if you're not going to even look at the basket."

Sir responds, "I'm just trying to include everybody—"

"Forget that! Play your game! Include us that way. Isn't leading by example what the best player does? Then lead! Or quit and let us figure it out without you. Cause right now, you're looking like some money is on the line," Eric says, continuing to walk onto the court leaving Sir, clenching his jaw.

"Walker brings the ball up," the sportscaster commentates. *"He puts a move on the defender. He shoots a step-back three... Swish! He makes his first shot of the night. Now let's see if that gets the Bison going."*

After Sir's basket, the Spartan's lazily inbound the ball. Sir intercepts the pass, euro-stepping around the rim protector for the score.

"Walker with a sweet move, scoring back-to-back baskets."

This not only pumps up his teammates, but it pumps up Coach Bradford as well, as he calls out for his team to press-up on the Spartans full court. Catching the Spartans off guard, they turn it over again. Sir penetrates to the basket and kicks to Eric, open in the corner. He shoots and makes the three. And just like that, the score has gone from a twenty-two-point deficit to sixteen.

As the game progresses, Howard, led by Sir, make play after play, closing the scoring gap with each possession.

With ten seconds remaining and down two, Peter grabs the defensive rebound. Coach Bradford calls for a timeout. While Michigan State's band blows their horns to a rhythmic tune, the crowd chants their fight song. Coach Bradford grabs his clipboard, in true Doc Rivers fashion, and draws up his first potential game winning play of the season.

"We're going to go 24-Dive", he says, looking up to see his very attentive players. "Eric, inbound the ball, and you and Sir, haul ass up court. I want the double screen at the quarter court mark. Have it set. No offensive foul. Tommy, set the screen for Sir, then set the back screen for Big Earl. When Sir comes off Big Earl's screen, Tommy you should be right there for Big Earl. When Sir turns the corner, Big Earl should be diving to the basket. At the same time, Eric, you should be coming off Peter's screen, flaring to the corner, and Peter popping out. Sir, you got options. Just like in practice. Somebody's going to be open. I'm trusting you to make the right choice. Win or lose, way to fight back fellas. But let's go get this win. 'Win' on three! One, two, three…"

With their hands gathered in the middle of the huddle, in unison, they yell out, "Win!"

Every spectator in the arena is on their feet when the referee's whistle blows. Eric inbounds the ball to Sir. Sir explodes up the court with the defender on his back and the clock ticking away. *Six seconds*, he comes off the double screen. Earl dives to the basket. Eric floats to the corner. Sir has the pull-up, but he elects to penetrate. *Three seconds.* The defense steps up. Earl is open for the lob.

"Walker throws a skip pass to Sanders, in the corner," The commentator reports.

Eric catches it with the defender running at him. *One second.* He shoots…

"Sanders makes it! The Bison win! The Bison win!" The commentator shouts over the silence of the home crowd as the Bison players and staff rush from the bench onto the Spartan's court, expressing their gratitude by attacking Eric and piling on top of him.

After the game, the sideline reporter stands by, hoping to catch one of Howard's star players for a postgame interview. Earl walks past first.

"Earl…" she calls out.

"Be blessed," he says, continuing off the court.

She's thrown off by Earl's response, and a tad embarrassed, but quickly shakes it off to catch Sir. "Sir…" She calls out. Sir stops to talk the reporter.

"First off, congratulations on the win," she says.

"Thank you," he smiles.

"Down twenty-two, with sixteen minutes remaining, you will your team back to put yourself in position to have a chance to win it at the buzzer, in which you all do. Take me through what was going through your mind on that last play."

As sweat pours down his face and panting, Sir breaks it down for her, "I wasn't playing my best a little more than half the game. I was just trying to get everybody involved. Overthinking. And it was Eric who told me to just play my game, and that's what I decided to do. So, in that last play, I was just thinking, 'Make the right choice, two or three,' and Eric was open, so it was only fitting that I give him a chance to win it for us, and here we are, with our first 'W' in the books. As a matter of fact, Eric…," he waves Eric over. "He's the one you should be talking too." Sir daps up Eric, "Good shot boy," then steps away.

Eric is all smiles as he steps in front of the microphone and camera, grateful for his first nationally televised live interview. He waves to the camera and says, "Hi mom!"

This makes the reporter laugh.

A few days later, back in D.C., Sir, Big Earl and Peter enter from the cold into Prince Jones Barbershop. The sounds of buzzing clippers and the smell of talcum powder awaken their senses. They'd all been here a few times before, since arriving to Howard, but this was their first time coming in as victors of their first collegiate win. In typical upbeat fashion, the barbers greet the three of them with great energy upon entry. "AYYYE," they all yell.

"It's Bell, Biv, Devoe," a barber jokes.

"Nah, they the new H-Town," another barber pokes fun.

"Nah, they're just coming off their first win and feeling good, so they're Tony! Toni! Toné! today," the youngest barber yells out as the shop starts singing, "It feels good, yeah…"

As the three of them laugh at the friendly jokes being directed at them, Peter leans over to Sir and asks, "Who is Tony! Toni! Toné!"?

"Man, some old R&B group, I guess," Sir shrugs.

"Congratulations on your win fellas," Pops says, smacking on a plate of chicken. "Didn't think y'all was gonna pull the comeback off, but you did."

"Thanks, Pops," the three of them respond, taking seats on the burgundy leather couch-like booth that stretches the length of the shop.

An older patron dressed in a pair of slacks and dress shirt chimes in, "Yeah the spread was plus six for y'all. I put up a little five hundred. My winnings are helping pay for this haircut. I definitely appreciate y'all covering my bet."

While Peter and Earl are not quite sure what any of this means, Sir perks up. "Well, the money line was plus two-twenty-five. Had you had more faith in us, you'd be up eleven hundred twenty-five dollars instead of just almost doubling your money," Sir educates.

Some of the barbers and patrons cut their eyes at one another, suspiciously, after hearing Sir's response.

"What you know about money lines and spreads, young fella?" the well-dressed patron asks.

"Ah, I know a little bit," Sir confidently responds. "But we appreciate you thinking we were gonna lose by less than six. Glad we could make you some money."

"Me too! Now, what you got on our haircuts?" Peter says, eying the gentlemen.

Pops, damn near, chokes on his chicken bone laughing at Peter's brashness. "I know that's right, young blood," he says.

About two hours later Pete, Earl and Sir, all freshly cut, make their way towards the exit and bid the barbers and the patrons farewell. After wishing them good luck and watching them drive off in their Uber, the thoughts the barbers had been holding onto for the last two hours, since Sir shared his knowledge about betting on games, explode from their mouths.

"If there was any doubt that the kid threw that state championship game, I now am positive he did," a barber yells out. "Good kid. But definitely took some money on that one."

And the thoughts from the others are unanimous.

Chapter 13 – All Love

Big Earl knocks on Coach Bradford's office door then peeks in, "You wanted to see me… Coach?" He says reluctantly, at the sight of his speech class professor, Professor Mayhorn, seated across the desk from Coach Bradford.

"Yes, come in and have a seat, Earl," Coach Bradford says, sternly. Earl sits at the desk next to Professor Mayhorn. He gives a half-hearted smile and nods at the professor, knowing he may be in some type of trouble.

"What's up, Coach?" Earl asks.

"Professor Mayhorn, here, tells me you're not doing so well in class. He tells me that while you're excelling in the work aspect of the class, you have not fulfilled the necessary requirements in completing your speeches, which account for half of your cumulative grade. Which means, if you don't complete them, then you cannot pass the class. Which would make you ineligible for the next semester. Do you understand?"

Earl squirms in his seat, as beads of sweat form on his nose. "I understand, sir. It's just that, I'm not comfortable, standing in front of the class, giving a speech."

"But those are the requirements to pass the class," Professor Mayhorn, chimes in.

"Isn't there something else I could, I mean…"

"Earl, I don't understand what the problem, is," Coach, interjects. "On the court, you're this bigger than life figure, performing in front of tens of thousands of people and millions watching on television, and at a high level, I might add. Don't tell me that standing in front of a class bothers you."

"It's not just that, it's umm… it's umm." Earl says, now sweating profusely. As he searches for the words to say, he begins to massage the temples of his head with his fingers. "It's umm…" He says again.

"Earl, are you alright, son?" Coach Bradford asks, concerned. Earl's breathing is quick and shallow. Neither man is sure what's happening. "EARL," Coach calls out. "Call 9-1-1," he demands to the professor, at the sight of Earl's limp body hitting the floor.

Moments later, an ambulance's siren is heard entering campus.

Beep... Beep... Beep... The hospital monitor plays to the beat of Earl's pulse as he's lying next to it in the hospital bed. His eyes peer open as he awakes to the sight of Sir watching from his bedside.

"Good to see you awake big fella," Sir says, smiling.

"How long have I been here?" Earl asks with a groggy voice.

"A few hours. Everybody's here, chilling in the lobby. Doctor said you had a panic attack. Said your convo with Coach and Professor Mayhorn is what caused it. What's wrong big fella? You okay?"

Earl is slightly embarrassed to have Sir see him like this. And he's even more embarrassed to tell him the cause.

"You're my brother, man, you can tell me anything," Sir says sincerely in an attempt to reassure Earl's trust.

A tear rolls down Earl's face, and his lip quivers as he thinks about how to tell Sir his problem. "You ever feel like the walls are closing in on you, and that they're gonna crush you, and there's nothing you can do about it?" Earl asks.

Sir nods his head, "Yeah, the day I lost the state championship game."

"That's how I feel when I have to talk in front of crowds of people or in front of a camera. I can be in front of people, I can laugh, I play ball, but the moment I have to talk, I panic. The room just gets smaller, I get sweaty, I feel like I can't breathe, and my heart beats out my chest. It started when I was a little kid. We used to have to do these Easter speeches in front of the church, and it was my turn. And I had practiced my speech over and over and knew it beginning to end. Right before I went up, my father grabs me by the shoulder, and he says to me, 'Don't embarrass me, son'. He didn't say, 'I'm proud of you of you' or 'You're gonna do good, son,' nothing encouraging. He says, 'Don't embarrass me.' Like that's what I wanted to do. And what did I do when it was my turn? I froze up. I couldn't remember not one word of that speech to save my life. My mouth became dry, and I started sweating... And my father says out loud, 'Well, we know who's not going to be a leader like his daddy!' And at that, the whole church began to laugh at me. And I ran off the stage while everyone laughed at me. I ran all the way to a park a few blocks away from the church, and that's the day I picked up a basketball. And in my church clothes, I took my anger out on every kid on the court. That's why I'm able to play the way I play. Cause it's my therapy. It allows me to be the leader that my father said I'm not. But for some reason, I can't shake that day the church laughed at me, to allow me to speak in front of crowds. Just the thought of having to is the reason I passed out inside coach's office. That's why I didn't want to take that class. And now if I don't pass it, then I won't be able to help y'all finish what we came here to achieve." Earl, stares at the lights in the ceiling, lost in thought.

"What if I help you," Sir says.

"How are you gonna do that?"

"To be honest, I really don't know. But I'm thinking we just have to find you something that you like talking about just as much as you like playing basketball. Something that makes you comfortable enough to want to say it to people. If not, maybe we can get you a medical excuse, cause we can't have you passing out over it. What's something that you like to talk about that you don't have to think twice about?

"Boycotting!"

"Huh?"

"Boycotting! After I didn't want to do anymore speeches, I learned about boycotting. I became fascinated with the idea and started researching historical boycotts and the people who led them. Man, I studied so many civil rights activists and their movements. So, the next time Easter rolled around, I staged a boycott at the church for the kids that didn't want to do an Easter speech."

"You did what?" Sir asks, shocked.

"Yeah, and I know everything there is to know about them." Earl exclaims.

"I think we might have to get you that medical exemption," Sir says smirking. "Ever since Kaepernick, boycotting has become a sensitive subject."

Earl laughs, "Maybe you're right."

"I'm gonna tell everyone that you're okay. If that's cool with you?" Sir asks, standing up from the chair.

"Yeah, that's cool. Normally, my mom would just pray with me in times like this, but our talk helped just the same."

"Well, I can't say that I'm the best at the whole praying thing, but if I'm ever in the position you're in, feel free to pray for me," Sir responds.

"Will do, bro," Earl says, with a light smile. As Sir crosses toward the door, Earl calls out to him, causing him to turn around. "And Sir… You know, in all my basketball accomplishments, it wasn't until my announcement to attend Howard that my pops finally told me he was proud of me." Earl and Sir both ponder momentarily on Earl's bitter-sweet accomplishment, Earl looks toward Sir at the door, "Thanks, bro." Sir smiles, pats his heart, then exits.

Chapter 14 – Who Am I?

Since the party earlier in the year, Sir and Alex have had several on-campus lunch dates and an occasional movie in her dorm room. Today, they're going on an official date exploring the nation's capital. Alex is in her 3rd year at Howard studying Sports Journalism, and as a part of the university's work program, she is a professor's assistant for the communications department. So, between studying, working, and doing community work with her sorority, her and Sir's schedules rarely match up for them to capitalize on anything fun off campus. With Sir having the day off, and her schedule being clear, Alex is taking Sir to visit one of her favorite places in the city—*The Smithsonian's National Museum of African American History and Culture.*

Sir has heard great things about this museum but hadn't visited a museum since he last visited The Museum of Science and Industry back home in Chicago as part of a sixth-grade field trip. Ever since then, any trip anywhere has been basketball related. So, he is definitely excited. More importantly, he is excited to be spending time with Alex.

Dressed for the occasion, Sir sports a hoodie with Obama's red, blue and white *Change* photo adorning it—a little something he picked up in Chicago, from one of the local shops. It is perfect for this tough, winter D.C. weather and a conversation piece, as Alex enquires about it and compliments it as soon as Sir hops in her car.

At six-foot-three, Sir easily stands out among the crowd as he and Alex approach the steps of the museum. Therefore, from the moment they stand in line to enter, through their walk-through security, and their arrival to the elevator to start the tour, Sir is being recognized and given mad love by the people of D.C. Some simply want to say "Hi", some want to shake his hand, and some want a photo for the 'Gram, while others want all the above. He cannot walk more than a few steps without someone coming up to him. Almost all of the people want to thank him and tell him how proud they are of him for being the first of his talent in modern day to give an HBCU a chance. This is all an overwhelming experience for Sir, but he is grateful for the love. This is the first time he is getting to see how he and

Earl and Pete impact the city beyond the sport and the school. Some of these people are not even basketball fans, but they know who he is, and they are telling him how inspiring he is and how they are praying for him. He humbly appreciates every one of them. He also notices how Alex is standing by, without a jealous bone in her body, even helping take photos of him with his fans, smiling the whole time. He appreciates that of her. Alex understands his movement is bigger than basketball, probably even more so than he realizes himself.

The tour begins with an elevator ride to the bottom floor and entering a dimly lit exhibition of slavery in the United States from its inception. From the battles over sugarcane to auctioning off black people like property, Sir begins to correlate it to the sport he loves to play, and how something so pure, a talent he works hard on everyday attempts to be sold to the highest bidder, just like slavery. He begins to fill empowered, knowing that he has done it differently. He thinks about Booney's words of insight on that spring morning in Chicago, and how it helped change the course of his life as he knows it. As he stares at the slave ships painted on the wall with the number of slaves that each one of them carried from their homeland to

America, he understands they didn't have a choice. So, he proudly embraces his choice of attending Howard, knowing it was his choice and his choice alone.

Sir turns to Alex, a few feet away from him, seeing the pain in her squinted eyes while she stares at a pair of rusted baby shackles. He walks over to her, in an attempt to ease the heaviness, and asks, "So what made you want to become a sports journalist major? You trying to become the next Lisa Salters?"

This makes her smile, as she answers, "Actually, yes. If I'm lucky. She's so dope!"

"What's so dope about her?"

"What's not? A Black woman holding her own as she interviews the world's elite athletes, grasping their respect and their attention with her mind and not her ass, as they search intimately for the answers to her questions. Any kind of woman that can hold that kind of court is without a doubt, dope."

"I ain't say she wasn't *dope*, Maya Angelou," Sir jokes. "I just wanted to know why *you* thought she was dope, that's all."

"I did get kind of deep on you, didn't I?"

"Just... A little bit."

"A little bit?" Alex demonstrates with her fingers.

"Yeah, a little bit," Sir jokes, mimicking her gesture. The two of them share a laugh, continuing to walk through the museum. "So, besides Lisa being your inspiration, why else do you want to be a sports journalist?"

Without hesitation, Alex responds, "Because I absolutely love sports and the story of an athlete's journey. It's all just fascinating to me. Take your journey for instance. You were the number one high school player in the nation, and you could've gone to any one of the elite programs in the country, but you chose Howard. That's fascinating. I mean who does that? That's a story the world is waiting to hear."

"I can see that," he nods his head. "Wait, are you interviewing me?"

"Not at all. Because if I were interviewing you, I'd come right out and ask, how much did they pay you to come here?"

"So, you think Howard paid me?"

"Yep, I mean, I think somebody paid you. Why else would the country's best high school player attend an HBCU?"

"Maybe I just came here in hopes of meeting someone like you," Sir flirts.

Although she's flattered, Alex gives Sir a strong side-eye, "If that was Peter's response, I maybe would've believed it. But not you."

Sir laughs, "Nah, but for real…" focusing in on a picture of a group of male slaves, standing on an auction block, "Sometimes we get so caught up in the game, that players unknowingly become slaves to it. And coming to Howard made me feel like I was breaking those chains."

"But you're still a part of a team. So, there's still some sort of control substance. Why not just quit basketball altogether if you feel like a slave to it?"

"Cause I love basketball too much to let it go. But when everybody in the country is offering you money to go to here and to do this and to do that, and you accept it, you're a slave to them."

"So, you've never taken any money from any schools?" Alex asks.

Shaking his head and staring blankly at the ground, Sir responds, "Nope, I've never taken money from any schools." He breaks his trance, looking up at her, masking his true thoughts with a smile.

"I must say, that is quite shocking," she says, thinking about her journey. "As much as my family struggled to get me here, I would've."

Maintaining his innocence, Sir shrugs. "You didn't get a scholarship?"

"I mean, there are academic scholarships we can apply for, but as far as a straight up scholarship for sports journalism, like you got for being a part of a team... Nada."

"Dang, that sucks."

"Who you telling? HBCUs barley have money to pay for all y'all's scholarships. That's why it was good for you, Peter and Earl to come here because already y'all have generated more money for the school than they have made in the last decade off the program. That means, more scholarship money available for my department and others."

"I never looked at it like that. These schools make billions of dollars off student-athletes, and the amateur level is the only level that we can't make them pay for the power we release to them. Guys in the pros, they may get told when they can or can't play, what team they have to play for, or what company to wear, but, at the end of the day, they get to name their price. Not us. At least not legally. So that's why I'm not mad at the student-athletes who take money. I just don't want that power over me."

"So, by choosing Howard, you feel that you're holding onto that power?

"Yep, I do. At least some of it."

"Can I ask you something else?"

"Sure." Sir says, worried-free.

"Were you this deep before you came into this museum, Malcolm?" She jokingly asks.

"Ahh, you got me." Sir smiles ear to ear.

"I hope you didn't think I wasn't." Alex laughs.

Sir's phone rings. He pulls it out, seeing that it's Percy. He ignores the call. Alex notices.

"Groupie?" She asks.

"Something like that," he mumbles. "There's a whole different world going on where I'm from. You break that story, and you just might be the next Lisa Salters.

Later that day, following their tour of the museum, Alex's gray Honda pulls up outside of the athletes' dorm. They see Peter walking by, nestled between two fellow female classmates, arms around both, cheesing and pouring on the charm. Behind Peter is Big Earl, walking shoulder to shoulder with another female. She's locked in on his every word. Alex and Sir jokingly narrate what they see.

"Look at Peter, probably telling them, 'You know I'm half black right?'" Alex says, mocking Peter's voice.

"Nah, he's telling them, 'You know, we look like an Oreo cookie right now, meaning we all look good together.'" Sir mocks.

"For sure he's saying that." Alex continues in Peter's voice, "'I'm saying, who don't like Oreo's?'" The two of them laugh. "And what's Earl saying?"

"Earl is definitely telling her something about the Bible. Something like, 'Jesus, died so that you and I can live…'"

"And sex before marriage is unlawful in God's eyes, unless you're a star ball player,'" Alex adds, laughing."

Covering his mouth with his fist, Sir cracks up, "Dang, you cold for that!"

"You know that's what he's saying," Alex replies. "Cause that's how y'all be thinking. Y'all guys will say any and everything so the narrative fits your agenda. No matter what it is."

"That's not true."

"Sure, it is!" Alex exclaims. "You've been telling me whatever you think I'd wanna hear, since the day you've met me, thinking—"

Sir leans over, and kisses Alex, mid-sentence. She's totally caught off guard but enjoys the taste of his lips, so she closes her eyes and continues to kiss him back.

Inches from Alex's face, Sir asks, "What were you saying about us ball players?"

At a loss for words, Alex stutters, "I was saying, um… That, um…" She sees Percy's name pop on Sir's phone. "Your phone is ringing."

Sir looks down and his mood changes at the sight of Percy's name. He immediately starts looking around.

"Is everything okay?" Alex asks, concerned.

"Yeah, everything is fine," Sir says, still with his head on a swivel. "Let's, um, connect when we get back off the road."

"Okay…" Sir hops out of the car. "Talk to you… later," she says to a closed door, sensing something is terribly wrong."

Back in Chicago, Sir's mom, Joy, exits her car dressed in nurse's scrubs. She opens her rear door, reaching for a couple of bags of groceries. Just as she rises up, with the bags in her hand, she's startled by the towering presence of Percy, standing over her.

"Oh, Percy, you scared the heck out of me!"

"Let me help you with those bags," Percy says, grabbing the bags from Joy's grasp.

As they enter Joy's home, Percy, walking behind Joy, suspiciously surveys his surroundings before sitting the grocery bags on the kitchen table as instructed by Joy.

"Thank you," She says, smiling, putting her groceries away. "What brings you by tonight?"

"Oh, I was just in the neighborhood," He smirks. "Thought I'd stop by and check on you, since our boy is no longer here."

"Well, I appreciate that. It's been different not having him around, but my job has been keeping me busy."

"How's that going?" Percy inquires.

"It's been going great," She responds, lighting up. "It's a blessing to be finished with school and finally making some real money."

"I hear that. How's our boy doing?"

"He's doing good. You haven't spoken to him?"

"Not as of lately. I've been calling him, but he ain't been answering my calls. I guess he's been busy."

Joy finds this odd as she knows Sir would never neglect returning Percy's calls. Then she starts thinking about how she hasn't seen Percy since the state championship game. And it crossed her mind, then, how odd it was that Percy wasn't around Sir at the McDonald's game, nor was he at Sir's press conference for his college announcement. When she asked Sir about it, he told her Percy was staying out of the light for the time being. Putting two and two together, she now realizes Sir has disassociated himself from Percy, but she decides to play it off as if she doesn't know. "Probably

so," she responds. "Since he's been gone, I haven't spoken to him that much

either, but I'm sure he'll call you back sooner than later." Further trying to

ease his mind, she says. "You've always been good to us, and we appreciate

all you've done."

Joy's response seems to have an opposite effect on Percy, though.

"Do you?" He asks. "Cause it seems that our boy has forgotten just how

good I've been."

"What do you mean?"

Percy scans the room. "This is a nice home you've got here, Joy. I'm

glad to see my money was well spent. Maybe that stays between us. Maybe

it doesn't. All depends on if and when our boy calls me."

"I think it's time for you to leave, Percy." Percy tilts his head to the

side, leering at Joy, looking like he's about to attack her. She quickly draws

a butcher's knife from the knife rack. "Get the hell out of my house!

NOW!" Joy yells.

Percy smirks. "You make sure he calls me. Enjoy your evening."

Percy crosses toward the door, exiting. After he's gone, Joy immediately runs toward the door, locking it. She then leans her back against the door, closing her eyes, sighing in relief that things didn't go any further.

Chapter 15 – Is It Easy?

Bundled in light winter jackets and team sweats, Sir, Peter, and Big Earl enter the downtown Atlanta Marriott, where the team is staying, returning from a late-night run for food with bags and drink containers from Krystal's.

"I'm telling you Pete, if these don't taste like White Castle's burgers, you givin' me my money back," Sir stresses.

"And I'm telling you, they're the closest thing to, if not better. Tell him Big Earl," Peter boasts.

"I don't know, Pete, White Castle's is in a league of its own," Earl proclaims.

"And you're supposed to be from the south… Talking about White Castle's. You'll see. Watch." Peter reiterates.

Earl and Sir cut their eyes at one another, smirking. As the three of them walk through the lobby, they spot Eric, Big Tommy, and a couple of their other upper-class teammates, cleanly dressed, heading toward the doors.

"And just where in the hell y'all going, all swagged out?" Peter interrogates.

"If you must know, my Slim-shadiness friend," Eric jokes. "This is Atlanta, and when one is in Atlanta, where must one visit, Big Tommy?"

"Compound, bayyybayyy!" Tommy sings.

"Compound is where it goes down," Eric repeats.

"Oh, Compound, the club? We're coming with!" Pete says.

"Oh, no, we are not 'coming with'," Eric mocks. "Y'all may be some All-Americans, but y'all are too young, too white, and too religious. We'll see y'all tomorrow at shoot- around." Eric and the others proceed past them.

"But you forget being and All-American has its perks. People recognize us and give us free things… like free entry." Sir bargains.

"And free drinks," Earl chimes in.

"And sometimes, free lap dances," Peter adds.

The upper classmen look each other, liking the sound of all of that, and conclude it might not be a bad idea letting the youngsters tag along.

"Y'all hurry up and get dressed," Big Tommy demands. Excitedly, the three of them break for the elevator.

The line to enter the club is poppin', which typically means the club is poppin'. After standing in line for about thirty minutes, the Howard players reach the front of the line.

The security guard, a short, buff dude, yells out in his Atlanta twang, "I.D.'s out! And there's a twenty dolla' charge."

Eric whispers to Peter, Sir and Earl, "Y'all be cool, let me holler at him."

Before Eric can say anything, the security guard looks at them and says, "What y'all some ball playas or sum'tin?" Then he recognizes the HBC-3. "Oh, snap! You're that dude, Sir Walker! And you're Big Earl! And you da' White boy!" Peter's grin quickly turns into a straight face—looking salty. "I got tickets to the game tomorrow! I couldn't miss the opportunity to see y'all play. That's some dope shit what y'all did. Respect! Aye, y'all

think I could get a pic wit' y'all?" He pulls out his phone.

"Sure," Sir says.

"Aye fam', you mind?" The security guard hands Eric his phone.

After they take the picture, he yells out to the cashier, "Aye, Shalisha!

Hook'em up—they good! Y'all good. Y'all go on in. And good luck

tomorrow."

Sir shoots Eric with the 'I told you' look. Eric smiles as they walk in.

The club is jumpin'! It's packed to capacity, as expected, with

beautiful, voluptuous women and dudes dressed to impress. Gold grills and

cleanly edged-up dreads can be found on almost every other person,

bobbing their heads and reciting lyrics to the throwback Lil' Jon track

blasting through the speakers. The hostess leads the guys through the throng

of club goers to a VIP table toward the back. This takes the guys by

surprise. "Compliments of the promoter," she says, as a pair of scantily

dressed bottle service girls, carrying four bottles of top-shelf liquor, adorned

with sparklers, approach their table. This was the kind of treatment they've all heard about and witnessed from afar, but tonight it was their reality, and they all were loving every minute of it so far.

With all their glasses filled, the guys raise them and toast to the good life and a history making season, while the DJ shouts them out over the speakers. None of them could've imagined the love they are getting. It is a good feeling for them all, and if it is just for one night, or for one week, or for one season, they know they are a part of something special.

Later in the night, Sir sits at the booth by himself, drinking a bottle of water, watching his boys enjoy themselves. As thoughts of his last encounter with Alex play in his mind, he cannot help but think about Percy's phone call and how it affected the moment for him. It's been a few days since he last talked to her, and he knows he should call her soon. As he pulls his phone out to text her, Eric approaches, sweating and fanning himself.

"Man, it is lit in here! And your boy, Pete, knows more rap than me! He goes hard for the culture."

"Yeah, Pete secretly grew up in the projects somewhere on the outskirts of Oregon," Sir jokes. "Or at least has a black, hood auntie, we don't know about."

"Facts!" Eric laughs. "You weren't lying when you said being an All-American has it's perks. I'm glad you all came."

"Me too. Tonight's been a good night for us."

"Indeed…" A silence lingers between the two of them, as they both stare into the crowd, bobbing their heads to the music. Finally, Eric says, "Can I ask you something?"

"Sure," Sir reluctantly says, anticipating Eric's question.

"Is it hard being you?"

"What?" Sir asks, surprised by the question. "A good ball player?"

"Nah, you know, being considered one of the best?" Eric asks, sincerely. "Cause me, I just go out there and play. Nobody expects me to go to the league, to make the game winning shot, to lead a team… just play. Yeah, I have those dreams, but it ain't my reality. It's yours. So, I'm wondering, with all the attention that you get and the expectations of you to perform, is it hard, being you?"

Being him is something he has ever thought about. It's not like he has a choice of who he is. He is who God made him to be, at least that's what he thinks. He is a kid with an exceptional talent, and he accepts everything it comes with because it's all he knows. As he ponders the question, his response is simple, "Nah, it's easy being me. What's hard, sometimes, is trying to be who everyone thinks I should be."

"Then why not just continue to be you?"

"Easier said than done. But that's what I'm trying to do."

"I hear that… You know that was my first game-winning shot in the four years I've been here? Really, it was my first real game-winner ever!"

"Word?"

"Yep, felt good, too! I know you could've threw it up to Big Earl, so I appreciate you helping me achieve that feeling. That was pretty cool of you. I guess you ain't so bad after all." He extends his hand."

Sir laughs, "I guess not," shaking Eric's hand. "Having each other's backs, that's what teammates are for, right?"

"I guess so," Eric smiles.

"I see you Big Fella!" The DJ says over the speaker, drawing all attention to Big Earl, bursting out dance moves in the middle of a circle of folks cheering him on.

Away from the club and in the packed arena, the cheering continues as Earl slams the ball over an opponent. He lands, screaming to the top of his lungs, "And one!" He then breaks out into a quick dance, followed by a bow and gesture of praying hands to his opponent. "God loves you," he says, putting an exclamation point on the game that has become out of reach for Georgia Tech University, who is down twenty-three points.

Earl's dance goes viral on IG, capturing 3 million views and counting in the first couple of hours. This is the tip of the iceberg for the team's popularity which coincides with Howard's massive run over the next couple of weeks.

The HBCU conference games are a cake walk for Howard's team, and the mid-major teams aren't much of a threat either. The team is exciting and playing very well. Home games at the Capital One center are packed to capacity with fans bleeding Howard-blue in the stands. And road games aren't much of a difference as fans come from all over to witness the magic of the Howard movement. They're rock stars—it's like they are at an advantage everywhere they go. They are *must see tv*, knocking off major programs in Texas, Florida, and Louisville with a record of nine and one and ranked eighteenth in the country.

The attention for Howard University is line no other. A popular late-night television host even mentions them in his opening joke. *"I don't know what's more spectacular, an HBCU basketball team dominating college basketball, or that they have a white guy helping them do it?"* he says.

And he is one of many. Everybody is talking about Howard University's basketball team and the HBC-3. As they rack up the wins, going from nine and one to twenty-four and one, and from eighteenth to fifth ranked in the country behind Duke, Kansas, Kentucky and UNC, their popularity grows more and more.

Fans wearing the HBC-3 t-shirts high-five other fans on the street. From D.C. to New York, to Houston, to California, they are the talk of the country. Over the last few months, they've been the topic of discussion at every barbershop, game night and family gathering. If you don't know who

Howard's basketball team is by now, then you must be under a rock. They are everywhere. And it is all because of three eighteen-year-old kids, with the mindset and courage to make a decision to do something that hadn't been done.

Chapter 16 – Blow the Whistle

As light snowflakes fall on the prestigious infrastructure of Howard's campus, following a break in class, Sir, Peter and Big Earl enter the cafeteria for a bite to eat. At this point, the school is on a high from how well their basketball team is doing. For the players, the feeling would be equivalent to being a member of the seventy-three and nine Golden State Warriors. And for the fans, well, what fans aren't stoked about a winning sport's team?

Nearing the end of the season, Howard is a sure lock to win their conference and the favorite to win their conference tournament. After all, they are undefeated in conference play so far. For the first time in school history and the history of all HBCUs, Howard will, undoubtingly, get an automatic bid into the NCAA tournament. So yes, the HBC-3 is feeling really good about what they've achieved so far.

Sir, Big Earl, and Peter exit the cold and enter the warmth of the building, laughing and joking about Earl's late-night road "Bible session" with a pair of females he met on the Christians Mingle app. Peter gets a text from one of his homeboys back home: "ESPN says ya boy Sir is foul," he texts, followed by the link to the ESPN video, titled *"Money for Walker."*

"Yo, Sir! What's going on, bruh?" Peter asks, showing Sir his phone. My boy just sent me this. What are they talking about?"

As Sir reads the headline, he looks up noticing the students in the cafeteria whispering and pointing at him.

"Look at the TV," Earl says. Sir looks across the room to see Percy on the TV doing an interview with ESPN with the words, *"Percy Daniels: Sir Walker's money man"* headlined across the bottom of the screen. The thump of Sir's heart beats in his ears as he walks closer to the television. The sportscaster is firing off his questions.

"So, you're saying you paid Sir to throw last season's Illinois High School Basketball State Championship?" He asks.

"Is a pig's... snout pork?" Percy arrogantly asks. "Yes, last season's state championship was one of many games that he and I fixed throughout his high school career."

"For money?"

"Absolutely, for large amounts of money," Percy boasts.

"Let me ask you this," the sportscaster leans in, "Did Howard University pay Sir Walker to attend their school?"

"Why else would you think the nation's top high school basketball player would go there? Money! No other reason behind it."

All eyes are on Sir, watching Percy destroy his character on national TV. A lump forms in his throat, his body becomes numb, and he stares blankly, having not had this feeling but only one time before in his life—the day he lost the state championship.

A student seated in the cafeteria is heard saying, "Look, 'Sir Cheating' is the number one trending topic on Twitter."

Earl breaks Sir's trance by placing his big hand on his shoulder. "It ain't true, is it?"

Sir turns, filled with fury and tears, "I'ma get at y'all later alright." Sir darts for the door, harboring rage in his heart and fire in his tear-filled eyes with each step.

"Sir!" Peter and Earl call out.

With compassion for Sir, Peter solemnly says, "Damn, not my ni-"

Earl quickly turns to stop Peter before he can finish. Peter catches himself, "My bad, bruh. It slipped. I was caught up in the moment." He rambles, "Come-on Big Earl, I'm with y'all all the time... Hip-hop made me do it."

Earl turns and shakes his head, more worried about his boy, Sir, than using the moment to teach Peter a cultural lesson.

Mobbing through the campus yard with the phone to his ear, Sir bellows into the phone. "Why would go on TV and lie on me like that?"

"You didn't think I was just gonna let you go and live your best life without me that easily, did you?" Percy fires back.

"Let me? You don't own me!"

"Oh, but I do. The bills I've paid. The clothes I've bought. All the games we've played together."

"I played those games, not you!"

"No, we played those games! You did what I said do and when I said do it. Yeah, you made the baskets, but the ball was always in my court. Tens of thousands of dollars that I have spent on you and your mother over the years and you think that you're just gonna go off to college and then the

NBA without me? Nigga, please! I own your little young ass! And if you want this, mishap, to go away and for me to say that I made this whole thing up, then you will continue to jump when I say jump, run when I say run, and shoot when I say shoot. Do we have an understanding?" Percy says with vigor.

"No."

"What'd you say, boy?"

"I said, no. Contrary to your belief, I own me. And we will never have an understanding again." Sir ends the call then takes off running through campus.

Inside AD House's office, Coach Bradford, with the weight of the world on his shoulders, sits across from him, as if he's in an interrogation room of a police station, or even worse—on trial for his life. Either way, it's not a comfortable feeling, especially for a Black man. "So, you don't know about any of this?" AD House asks.

"How could I?" Coach Bradford responds defensively. "And besides, it doesn't matter what he did in high school, it doesn't have anything to do with his association with this program."

"It has everything to do with this university. It goes against everything we, at Howard, stand for."

"Sir said he didn't do what he's accused of, and I believe him. He sure didn't get any money from anybody here. And you know that."

"Then what is this Percy guy talking about?"

"I don't know! He's obviously lying. No one here has even heard of him before."

"But Sir knows him."

"So? You can't fault the boy for who he knows." Coach says, irritably.

"So, that doesn't fare well with our boosters, which puts me in an awkward position where a decision has to be made. With all the recent bribery scandals and allegations of shoe companies taking care of these athletes and their families, the NCAA isn't taking any chances, and neither are we."

"Tim, what does that have to do with Sir? No one gave him any money to come here."

"It has everything to do with Sir. Obviously, he's caught up in this somehow." AD House pauses. "The NCAA and I have agreed that the best thing for the brand and program would be to suspend Sir for the remainder of the season. So that's what has happened."

"You did what?" Coach Bradford sits up in his chair. "Without a proper investigation? Are you kidding me? Over some hear-say? With four games left in the season and the conference tournament approaching?"

"I'm sorry, Corey. The NCAA has a rule called the Restitution Rule, and if we go against their decision, then they can forfeit all games that he's played in as well as adhere future punishments to the university. And we can't have that. We all have to cover our necks."

"Clearly! That's all folks in your position ever do. I don't believe this. Thanks for nothing, Tim," Coach says, headed for the door. He stops and turns around. "Was it faring well with the boosters when they were getting all that attention because of Sir and fattening their and the school's pockets? And the NCAA, don't get me started on them! What I wanna know is, at what point do we stop trying to cover our own necks and start showing that we really do care about these kids and what happens to them in the midst of all of this brand protecting that they're helping build? Have a good day, Tim." Coach says, storming out.

Having not been able to reach Alex since the scandal broke, Sir sits with is head buried between his legs, in front of her dorm room door, waiting for her to come. After two hours pass, Alex strolls up. Sir hops to his feet.

"Hey, what's up Alex?"

"What are you doing here, Sir?"

"I've been calling you all day. Why haven't you returned my calls?"

"Why'd you have to lie to me?"

"I didn't lie to you," Sir says, with agitation, yet sincerely.

"I asked you have you ever taken money from a school, and you told me no. You looked at me and lied to my face."

"I didn't lie. I've never took money, from any school. That's the truth."

"That ain't what Percy Daniels is saying."

"Who cares what Percy says!" Sir exclaims, raising his voice, then, catching himself as a pair of students walk by. "Percy is the one that's lying."

"Oh, so some guy that you don't know goes on TV and tells the world that he gave you tens of thousands of dollars to throw a game and to come here? Please."

"I never said I didn't know him. Nor did I say I never took money from him."

"So, which is it? Did you or didn't you take money from the school?" Alex asks, crossing her arms.

"I told you that there are some things that go on in my city that you wouldn't believe. And Percy is the brains behind it all. He's brought Vegas to Chicago high school basketball. And while I did some things to get money from him, I did not do the things that he said I did. So no, I didn't lie to you. I just didn't elaborate on the truth. You believe me, don't you?"

"I don't know, Sir," Alex says with a blank stare and feeling embarrassed and hurt. "I just need some time to process all this, because at this point, I don't know what to believe. Excuse me." She says, opening her room door.

"Alex," Sir calls out, reaching for her arm. She gently pulls away and shuts her door.

Feeling like his life is over and he has let everyone down, Sir sits in the bleachers of the football field alone with his phone to his ear, listening to the comforting sound of his mother's voice.

"You've been through worse," Joy says. "You just have to weather the storm and trust that God is still in control. Do you hear me?"

"I hear you."

"I mean it. You're going through this because God has something special just for you."

"And He couldn't find no other way to give it to me?"

"No, because tests and trials come to make you strong. You just hold your head up, son. He didn't bring you this far to leave you. You wait and see. When this is over, you will be stronger and better. And be prepared, because the victory you're going to receive from this situation is going to be far greater than you could ever expect."

Before making the call to his mom, Sir knew that despite the pain he was feeling, his mom would be able to ease it, even if just for a little bit.

The next day, all of the Howard players, minus sir, sit in the bleachers of Burr Gymnasium as Coach Bradford and his coaching staff stand before them. It's a solemn feeling. You would think they're record was one and twenty-four instead of the other way around. Coach Bradford addresses the team about Sir's situation, the best way he knows how. "I'm sure everyone has heard by now that the NCAA has suspended Sir from the team until further notice," he says. "The NCAA is going to do an investigation on the situation at hand, and when they conclude they will let us know if and when Sir can return."

"And when is that, Coach?" Peter asks.

"Who knows. Hopefully sooner than later."

"They can just do that," Earl questions "suspend a player because of some allegations?"

"Well, the school has decided it's in the program's best interest to do so—"

"But what do you think?" Earl interjects.

Though feeling like the players, Coach Bradford chooses to give un-biased answer. "I think that we should stay focused and try to finish what we've started."

Earl stands to his feet. "Coach, with all due respect, how are we gonna finish what we've started if the person who started this all, ain't even here to finish it with us? He said he didn't do it, and I believe him."

"What about the rest of you?" Coach asks the rest of the team. The players nod their heads in agreement.

"Sir ain't no liar, Coach," Eric chimes in. "And he ain't no cheater, either. I used to want to believe differently, but once I got to know him, I now know differently. And that ain't him."

Coach Bradford is speechless as he proudly stares at a group of guys that he has watched, over the last few months, go from not passing the ball to one another, to banding together through brotherhood as a team does.

Chapter 17 – Slave to The Game

Up six, with less than two minutes remaining, despite not having their star, the Bison have managed to control *this hard-fought game.*" The TV commentator announces, following a bucket by Big Earl. *"This is the Bison's closest scoring game in the conference, as they have been running through the MEAC, effortlessly, winning each game by an average of eighteen points."*

"No doubt, they're a little out of tune. And it's expected, without they're their floor leader tonight. But I tell you, that Mr. Big Earl Singleton has come to play, leading the charge all night," the *other* commentator chimes in.

Eric makes a move and throws the alley-oop to Big Earl. He misses the lay-up but quickly recovers the ball, pounds his defender, then dunks on him—and one! Big Earl shows no emotion at all, barely high fiving his own teammates.

"And on cue, Big Earl unleashes the beast!"

"Yes, he did! That was a grown man move right there, scoring his 25th point of the night."

After making the free-throw, Earl runs back on defense and blocks the opponent's shot into the stands, then stares down his opponent like boxers do right before the start of a fight. The whistle blows and the referee yells out, "Technical foul. Number thirty-two. Taunting."

Earl reacts to the call. "Tech on me? That's cute. God bless you too," he says, on his way to the bench, while the crowd boos the call. "Sub me out coach. I'm done for the night."

"You okay Big Fella?" Coach Bradford asks.

"They don't want us to play. It's obvious. Calling bad calls all night. I'm good," Earl says sitting on the bench, untying his shoes.

The buzzer sounds, ending the game, and Earl marches toward the locker room. A reporter and a cameraman chase behind him.

"Great game tonight. You were playing like a mad man for your team. With highs of twenty-six and seventeen, and Sir out until further notice, is this the type of play we can expect from you to help your team finish off the season and enter conference tournament play?" The reporter asks.

"No comment. Be blessed," Earl says continuing to walk. After walking away several steps, Earl returns to the reporter. "Tonight's game was played out of pure frustration on my behalf as a result of what my friend and teammate, Sir, is going through. I think it's wrong what is happening to him. I personally didn't want to be out there without him. And it pisses me off knowing that he's been stripped from doing what he loves and that he has to watch us play all because he's being treated as guilty until proven innocent instead of it being the other way around—just like every athlete in this country. And every time I ran up the court tonight, I felt as if I wasn't standing up for him, like I know he would stand up for me, going against the whole reason we even came to this school, together, in the first place. Coming here and playing without him means nothing if we're not finishing what we started. And I just can't do it anymore."

"Are you saying you're not going to finish the season without Sir?" She asks.

"That's exactly what I'm saying. If my brother can't play, then neither will I. To hell with a Restitution Rule. I'm done," Earl says, walking off, leaving the reporter with her mouth open in shock.

News has hit the fan about the statement Earl made after last night's game, and the media is in a total uproar the following morning. With Coach Bradford running around like a chicken with its head cut off, putting out fires in the form of interviews and press conferences, the entire team has gathered in Burr Gymnasium to add a bit of fuel to the flame.

After an intense moment of silence following the team's breaking news, Sir stands to his feet, pleading with his teammates, "Look guys, I appreciate what y'all are doing, but I can't let y'all go out like this."

"And unfortunately," Eric responds, "You don't have a choice, my guy. We're all with Big Earl on this one. If they're not letting you play, then none of us are playing."

"That's right," Peter adds. "We're brothers. And brothers ride with each other, no matter what it is."

Tommy chimes in, "Especially when it's for the right cause. If we continue to play without you, then they'll continue to do this to whoever, whenever they want to. And we ain't letting that happen. Not anymore."

"If they're gonna 'Kaepernick' you from college basketball, then they're gonna have to 'Kaepernick' us all," Peter says.

"That's right," Earl adds. "We've been the show of the year, and everybody's made all this money off of us, so we're gonna show them what we're really worth."

"So, y'all really about to do this?" Sir asks.

Eric responds, "Nah, *we're* really about to do this. We may not be able to fight it in court, but we don't have to play either. It ain't like we're losing any money. And if we were, then so be it. Like Coach said, we're a team."

Unbeknownst to the team, Coach Bradford has been standing outside of the locker room listening the entire time. He sighs in worry, then walks off.

After a long day and coming to terms with what the team has decided to do on his behalf, Sir stands before the trophy case and display that honors his late grandfather. He stands there thinking about what his grandfather might do in this situation, and he decides to read his grandfather's letter:

Slave to the Game, by Aldis 'Sir' Walker

For four hundred years, black people were enslaved in this country that we've grown to love, fight for, and die for. We were taken from our motherland, separated from our mothers, fathers, sisters, brothers, wives, husbands, and kids. We were stripped of our pride and dignity, beaten, raped, and killed. We were told when to speak, when to eat, when to sleep, among other things. We worked tirelessly in the hottest weather conditions for no pay. And when our, 'masters' wanted to use us for their amusement and entertainment, we jumped when they said 'jump', we danced when they said 'dance', and we even fought one another when they said 'fight'.

It's all these reasons and more why I refuse to play the game that I cherish and fell in love with as a kid, to bring profit to an institution that was built on the backs of my oppressed ancestors cultivated with their blood, sweat, and tears. I will not play for the benefit of people who ultimately despise because of the color of my skin. I will not be anyone's slave. If I'm going to go out there on the court and give my all to the game that I love for free, then I'm going to do it for my people and at an institution that was built for my people, understands my people, and has the best interest of my people at heart. If any money is going to be made from my talent, at least I know that money is going back into my community for my people.

I'm going to enjoy winning games with those who look like me and I'm going to cherish the times we'll cry over losses. I can imagine the unity on campus, and how great it will feel walking past and sharing classes with those who are cut from the same cloth as me and who can relate to my struggle along with teachers and faculty who understand that the color of my skin is not a threat. A slave to the game, I will not be. I'm free. And enjoying the freedom of playing the game of basketball is what I want for myself. Nobody owns me. This is why I have declined the offer to play for the blue-blood school that shall remain nameless, and I have decided to accept a full ride to play for Howard University.

Sir is filled with emotion as he sits with his grandfather's words resonating within his soul. If he wasn't sure before, he now knows the real reason he is supposed to be here. As he stares on, he hears footsteps behind him. He turns around.

"Powerful words, aren't they?" Coach Bradford asks.

"Yeah. Who would've thought something my grandfather wrote fifty, or so, years ago would be the blueprint of my life today?" Sir replies.

"Life is funny like that, sometimes."

"You know, this is my first time reading this letter?"

"It is? You didn't read it when I sent it to you?"

"Nope."

"So, what made you call me that night and decide to come here?"

"The same reason my grandfather did fifty years ago. It just felt right in my heart. And I needed to let the world know that I'm in control of me, and no one else."

"Look Sir, I don't know why God chose me to be the one that you decided to share this experience with, but whatever happens, I just want you know that I appreciate you. And I'm sorry you're going through this."

"Yeah, me too. But it is what it is, I guess," Sir shrugs. "Aye Coach, there's something I need to tell you."

"I'm listening."

"The team has decided to boycott the rest of the season."

"Yeah, I know. I overheard you guys talking earlier."

"You did? I'm sorry, Coach."

"Don't be. I'm not. Nothing changes if nothing changes, right? And if we're going to change how things are done, then doing it together is how we're going to do it. So, a boycott it is."

Chapter 18 – All or Nothing

The Capital One Arena is packed to capacity with restless fans who have seen no sign of the home team. Their opponent has finished warming up and is sitting on the bench, waiting with the rest of the world, for the Bison to take the floor so the game can start. Everyone is perplexed, especially since the team was seen entering the arena.

"In unfamiliar fashion," the commentator addresses the audience watching on TV, *"The Bison have yet to come out of the locker room to warm up, and we're seconds away from the scheduled tip-off."*

"Well, freshman center, Earl Singleton, did say he wasn't playing anymore until Sir was back. You don't think the rest of the team has decided the same, do you?" The *other* commentator asks.

"If they did, then they sure did pick a peculiar time to do so, being that we're live and nationally televised."

The horn sounds, and the opposing team hesitantly takes the floor. Murmurs fill the arena. Sitting in the crowd, AD House, is putting on face, for his guest, Mayor Townsend. But at this point, even he is dumbfounded.

A few minutes later, a professionally dressed woman emerges from the tunnel, and makes her way to the scorer's table, carrying a note. She hands the note over and proceeds to walk away. After reading the note and passing it around the table, a representative of the arena grabs a microphone and takes center court to make the announcement. As he does, the commentator addresses those, watching from home. *"Well fans, it's been confirmed. The entire Howard Bison basketball team is refusing to take the court. They're boycotting the rest of the season."*

Frenzy floods the stadium. AD House, with fire in his eyes, excuses himself from the mayor and marches straight for the locker room.

Thunderous banging on the door penetrates the locker room where the players and coaching staff sit in silence.

"Corey, you come out here *right now!*"

AD House demands.

"Well, fellas. It has begun," Coach Bradford says as he stands and makes his way to the door. He comes out to Tim cursing at the security guard for not allowing him to enter as he was instructed.

"How can I help you, Tim?" Coach Bradford asks.

"What do they mean, they're not playing anymore?" AD House insists.

"Just like the note said, until Sir is able to play again, they're willing to sit out with him."

"You were supposed to convince Earl to continue to play, not lose the rest of the team in the process."

"I didn't lose them, Tim. I'm with them. And if you were with Sir, having his back, then maybe we wouldn't be in this predicament."

"Do you realize how much money our school is losing? The NCAA will have our ass! This is a nationally televised *game*," AD House exclaims.

"I know. I saw the schedule. But that's your concern. These kids are mine," Coach Bradford says, then confidently walks away.

"Corey, your job is at stake here!"

"I'm sure it is, Tim. I'm sure it is."

A few states south of D.C, down in Durham, North Carolina, the distinguished and top ranked Duke men's basketball team sits around their crème de la crème locker room, preparing to take the floor for their game. Some are getting last minute ankle wraps and others are doing their final stretches when phones begin vibrating from inside their lockers.

One of the players, standing up at his locker, checks his phone and reads an ESPN alert. "Aye, y'all check this out," he yells out. "The whole Howard basketball team is boycotting the rest of their season."

"No way," another player shouts, grabbing for his phone. The players start grabbing for their phones, to see the news for themselves. They begin yelling out different things they're reading.

"Says they're not playing without Sir, and they're sitting with him for being wrongfully suspended."

"They're calling it 'The Sit Down.'"

"The Sit Down?"

"Yeah, it's all over social media. Other schools' players are doing it too."

As the Duke players discuss what the Howard team is doing, Rick

sits among them in a daze, biting his bottom lip, thinking about the phone

call he had the night before with Sir:

"What do you mean, you want me to join y'all?" Rick asked Sir.

"Exactly what I said," Sir responded. "We need you and your team's

help in boycotting the NCAA on my behalf and for other players in similar

situations so this can stop happening."

"Our next game is against UNC, Sir. The biggest game of the college

season! I need this game. And I need the others after it. My season ain't

been as good as yours, and you know that. I'm a late first rounder at this

point, at best. And you want me to join you in shutting down the rest of the

season which could possibly lead to no NCAA tournament? I can't do that

Sir. Not if I wanna be a lottery pick. I need to ball out."

"Man, you know those mock drafts ain't the be-all and end-all.

You're on the number one ranked team in the nation. It's full of talent. NBA

scouts know that. They also know your game."

"That's easy for you to say, Sir. You're number one on everyone's mock board. I'm not. Why do you even care? Just sit out, work on your game and get drafted. That's the whole reason we play ball anyway, right?"

"My name is on the line, Rick! If I do that, it's basically admitting to the things Percy said I did, and you know they ain't true! I ain't did nothin' you ain't you did. We did what we did, together. Everything."

"I ain't never throw no games, Sir."

"And I did?" Sir responded in shock.

"I don't know what you did, my guy. All I know is P on TV sayin' some things that seem a little suspect to me. I never asked you what happened in our last game. Hell, you've made it so nobody could ask you nothin' after that. You just been doin' your own thing—"

"I've been breaking the chains, that's what I've been doin'," Sir interjected.

"Sir, you my brother, and all, but I gotta look out for me like you been lookin' out for you." Rick said, with the utmost respect for his lifelong friend.

"Break them chains, bro. That's all I'm sayin'. Break them chains and help us change the game. Just know, we're doin' it with or without you." Having had enough of trying to persuade Rick to see things differently, Sir ended the conversation with, "I'm a holla at you," and then hung up his phone.

Rick looks up from replaying the conversation in his mind. His attention is drawn back to his team as one of the players calls out to him, "Yo, Rick, what's up with your boy Sir and them? They wild'n!"

Rick responds, "Nah, they're changing the game. That's what they're doin'."

After talking to Sir on the phone, Rick thought about all the things he and Sir had been through together as boys, and how Sir always had his back no matter what. Although he is not sure of what actually transpired the day of their championship game, he knows Sir is not a liar and Percy is more than capable of fabricating a story. '*I did what you did*' plays in Rick's mind like a song on repeat. He genuinely holds a mountain of respect for Sir for choosing to attend Howard. Truth be told, he wishes he would've been bold enough to do it himself. Now that an opportunity to make a bold move to stand strong with his brother stares him in the face, he will not back down. Unbeknownst to him, many others are standing strong also. Sir and his teammates have reached out to several of their friends on teams throughout the country, informing them of their boycott and asking them to join in. And more than enough have given their word they will.

"I just got a message, asking me to join in on 'The Sit Down,'" a Duke player says.

"Me too," another says. "They don't really expect us to participate in this, do they?"

"Yeah, they do," Rick shouts. "And we have to. It's the only way stuff is going to ever change for us."

"But we got UNC, tonight!" A player exclaims.

"All the more reason why we must do it too," Rick says, standing to his feet. "Howard is us, just in a different uniform. Look at what they've done this year. They've gone from nobodies to a top ranked school in a matter of months. They're not just some team. They're the 'Fab Five' of our time, maybe bigger. They're a movement—the statement of our generation. And I don't know about y'all, but it's somethin' that when I look back twenty years from now, I wanna say that I was a part of it. So, if they're sitting down, then so should we." Rick takes a seat. "Now y'all can join me if y'all want, or y'all can be the next victim of the Restitution Rule and afraid to fight back when some person lies on you."

"Why he ain't lie on you? You're from Chicago too. Sir must've done what he said, right?"

"I know Sir, and I know he's done what he's had to do. But I know he wouldn't go out like that. So, I'm ridin' with him."

A few players take a seat next to Rick, but the majority exit the locker room and head to the court to play in the game. Rick watches with the few as the majority leave, nervously contemplating his decision.

Da-da-da! Da-da-da! The ESPN theme song plays right before the sportscaster takes center stage, live from the ESPN studios, addressing a national audience. *"In entertainment, we've seen the actors and writers strike. In professional sports, we've seen the lockouts. We've seen kneeling for racial injustice. We've seen fists raised for Black pride. Today, we've experienced The Sit Down, an unprecedented protest in amateur sports…"*

Chapter 19 – The Sit Down

With Burr Gymnasium in his background, an onsite reporter for the local news channel holds his network represented microphone, speaking into the camera. *"As we approach March Madness,"* he reports, *"The NCAA is dealing with complete chaos as more than twenty-five hundred men and women basketball players and at least sixty-two complete teams have committed to The Sit Down which started just a few days ago, right here in D.C., when the Howard Bison men's basketball team vowed to sit out with their teammate, Sir Walker, who was suspended once news broke that he allegedly took money to attend Howard University and throw basketball games when he was in high school. According to the student-athletes around the country, a message was sent out asking them to join the movement and discontinue playing until Sir Walker is again granted the right to participate in collegiate sports. The Sit Down stems from amateur athletes who are tired of seeing fellow athletes lose their ability to participate because an NCAA rule was broken, and/ or they were found guilty before* having *the chance to prove their innocence. And because of the NCAA's Restitution Rule, that's designed to make them above the law, even if said athlete takes their case to court and happens to win and be reinstated by the school, the NCAA could potentially penalize the school in the form of forfeiting victories, surrendering television revenue,* imposing *fines, etc. On one side of the debate, student-athletes participating in The Sit Down, feel it is unfair their talent rakes in hundreds of millions of dollars a year for universities, while they receive no compensation. And, if the Sir Walker allegations are true, they would not fault him.* However, the NCAA, on the other side of the debate, argues the integrity of the game is at stake. *If Sir Walker cheated in high school, it is likely he is cheating on the collegiate level—something that will not be tolerated. If he has accepted money to attend Howard University, he is in clear violation of NCAA rules. But again, nothing has been proven. Since it is Sir Walker's word against the man making the claim, the question remains… why is Sir not being allowed to play?"*

"Power, that's why," a Howard student answers the question via his social media page. *"If he did or didn't take the money, the NCAA doesn't like anybody making money besides them. If they paid these players that have turned them into a multibillion-dollar organization, then they wouldn't have to worry about who's guilty of accepting money from schools and outside individuals. But they don't want to share the wealth, so they have set rules against those who want to go out and get it for themselves."*

Another student, takes to his page, *"It's about time a group of individuals started recognizing their power and standing together for what they believe is right so that they can make a difference."*

"I was with Sir and them when they all decided to go to Howard together. But now they got teams quitting. Messing up March Madness. Straight BS!" a fan stresses.

"When Ali stood his ground on the Vietnam War, I wish other boxers and athletes would have joined him like these athletes are joining Sir. Maybe it would've allowed Ali to keep his belt and stay out of jail like I believe this act of solidarity is going to get Sir back on the court," a blogger says.

"Of course, it's going to make a difference," a female student responds to the reporter on campus. *"These schools, the NCAA, and the networks are losing tens of millions of dollars. Why wouldn't it make a difference?"*

In Indianapolis, home of NCAA headquarters, a perturbed employee snatches a piece of paper entailing the reported boycott numbers from his printer. He rushes the paper down to the corner office of the gray-haired commissioner and hands it to him. The commissioner takes a look at the paper, unfazed.

"Are these numbers accurate?" the commissioner asks.

"Looks like it. Forty-one hundred basketball players and ninety complete teams and counting… men's and women's."

"We're three days away from the start of conference tournament play."

"On the bright side, there are still four hundred eighty-two men's and women's teams left, and that's in most of the major conferences."

"Good."

"But even the majority of those teams are down to six, seven players. The most a team has is nine."

"Well that's not a total loss. We'll still have games to fulfill our TV obligations. Let's just hope it doesn't get any worse," the commissioner says, perking his eyebrows and sipping his coffee.

The employee pauses, staring at the commissioner with a look of concern.

"What is it?" The commissioner asks.

"Um, more than fifty-six thousand athletes from the other sports have joined in on The Sit Down. And that's just division one."

The commissioner chokes on his coffee, "Oh, you're just full of great news today, aren't you?"

Coach Bradford's upper body sits stiffly in his chair as he slowly rocks the base of it from side to side with his legs. He holds an extended stare at his computer screen, almost staring through it as he remains in deep thought.

"Coach," Jannette, the secretary says, peeking her head into the office. "You probably need to check your email and schedule a meeting with the University President as soon as possible."

"Not before scheduling a meeting with me first," AD House interrupted authoritatively seeming to appear out of thin air. A rare sight in Coach Bradford's office, his presence suffocates the room. "You're about to earn that paycheck now."

Not aware what either of them is talking about, Coach Bradford opens his email and sees an unread message from Nike marked as *urgent*. It's addressed to himself, Tim House and the University President.

"Greetings:

Being that we are amidst a super sensitive moment in the NCAA that will call on society to be the court of opinion, we at Nike want to reiterate and reinforce our policy as it pertains to protest and freedom of speech from our member institutions. We welcome it. We encourage it. We celebrate it.

However, and most importantly, we mandate that all instances of protest involving athletics be applied toward proper matters in the most effective manner, and we must consult you in the process. As the sponsor

of your men's basketball team, not adhering to our policy is a breach of

contract, and all benefits within are at risk. We will allow you to discuss

internally, and then schedule a time to speak collectively."

"Oh shit," Coach Bradford says in a sigh under his breath.

"That's right, oh shit," AD House says. "So, young lady, before

scheduling any meetings with the University's President, allow Coach and I

to have a moment."

A few days later, marquees outside college arenas and gyms across

the nation disappoint faithful fans, displaying the message: *"Conference*

Tournament Cancelled".

The NCAA commissioner stands at the podium ahead of hundreds of

eager news reporters, answering questions about the situation as they pour

in.

"Bob Franklin, ESPN News," the reporter says, standing to his feet.

Commissioner, with all the sit downs and conference tournament games

cancelled, how do you think this will affect the NCAA tournament?"

"Well, I guess it's going to be one hell of a Selection Sunday," The commissioner jokes. The reporters laugh.

"But seriously, how serious is the NCAA taking this matter now with hundreds of millions of dollars in revenue being lost, and now, a whopping two hundred sixty thousand athletes are refusing to participate?"

"Our best interest is always the student-athletes, so we, the NCAA, have reached a verdict to give Sir Walker a chance to appeal to the NCAA on his behalf to defend the allegations against him"

"Just an appeal? So, what happens if the NCAA finds him guilty?"

"That's a road we'll have to cross when we get there. All in all, we hope the student-athletes recognize the NCAA's endeavor to make this process as fair as possible for Sir Walker and are willing to end the boycott and continue with the season regardless of the outcome."

"Why wasn't Walker granted the opportunity to appeal Mr. Percy Daniel's accusations before he was suspended?"

"Well, had we known it was going to come to this, we would have," the commissioner says grinning, "but this type of accusation is a matter we take very seriously here at the NCAA and have dealt with such circumstances before. So, we felt it was in our best interest and the program of Howard to suspend Walker while we investigate the matter. Therefore, if he is found guilty, we wouldn't have to forfeit their entire season."

"When can we expect this appeal before the board to happen?"

"We're making arrangements now to fly Walker and his mom to Indiana as we speak so that we can make it happen in the next day or so."

Sitting in their dorm room watching the NCAA commissioner on television, Peter turns to Sir and Big Earl and says, "Damn, we really shut down the NCAA! Man, you should've demanded some money!" They all laugh.

"You thought about what you're going to say in your interview?" Earl asks.

"I'm not gonna do it," Sir responds.

Earl and Peter quickly turn their heads toward Sir. "You, what?" They ask, confused.

"Isn't this what we did this for—for you to get an opportunity to play?" Peter questions.

"Yeah, dawg, wassup?" Earl asks.

"That's still on their terms, which means that's still under their control. This whole journey has been about empowering who we are and what we're worth. And I'm not about to let them diminish that by sitting me in some room while they judge me with their questions that they have already pre-determined the answers to. They don't know me. They don't know us. All they know is that we made them a whole lot of money and then stopped them from making it. If I'm going to tell my story, our story, I'm going to tell it in my own way."

The fellas look at Sir as if he's crazy. But they've gone this far and there is no way they are going to turn back now.

"All right, so what's the plan?" Earl asks.

Just then, there's a knock at the door. Peter gets up to answer it. "What's up, Al!"

"Hey, Pete," Alex greets. "Is Sir here?"

Peter looks behind the door for Sir's approval. He nods, then heads toward the door.

"What's up Alex," Sir greets her with a dry tone. This is the first time they've spoken in several days since their last conversation outside her dorm room door.

"Can we talk?" She asks. The two of them walk out in the hallway. "I guess you really do have a bit of Malcolm X in you," she jokes to sort of break the ice. "Almost three hundred thousand athletes have given up their varsity letters for you."

"Yeah, I didn't ask them to. This whole thing was actually Earl's idea."

"But they did it for you," Alex exclaims. "Everybody believes Percy Daniels is lying on you."

"Yeah, everybody but you."

Alex drops her head, embarrassed. "That's why I'm here. I want to apologize for the way I handled the situation. I just figured your situation was like every other blue-chip athlete and that you couldn't be honest with me about it."

"But I was, though. I have no reason to lie to you. Look where I am. My situation is far from every other blue-chip athlete's. I came to Howard cause I wanted to, not because somebody paid me to. I needed you to believe that. I needed you believe in me," Sir pleads.

"I know you did, and I'm sorry I didn't. I hope you can forgive me for it?" She says, sincerely, grabbing his hand.

Standing in tension-filled silence, feeling her warm, soft hand clutching his, Sir stares down the hallway pondering the matter. Alex is someone he knows he can genuinely trust, but she just made the mistake of not trusting him. Although it hurt him, he understands why she didn't. He just wishes she'd handled it differently. Finally, he breaks the tension with a smile.

"Of course, I forgive you," he says. At that, she smiles back and hugs him. "Did you hear?" Sir asks.

"Hear, what?" She questions.

"The NCAA is granting me a hearing to see if they're going to allow me to play again."

"No, I didn't. That's great!" She exclaims.

"Yeah, but I'm not going to do it."

"Wait, what? Why not?"

"Because… if they want my story now, they're going have to hear it via the best up and coming sports journalist."

"What does that mean?" She asks.

"It means that I want you to interview me. Allow me to tell you my story via Facebook Live, or something. And the NCAA board can make their decision from that. Save me the agony of sitting in a room with a bunch of suits that want me to be guilty."

"Sir, are you serious?" She asks as her stomach nervously rumbles.

"I'm as serious as my suspension, ma," he says, looking at her with a great deal of confidence.

After taking a deep breath, Alex responds with the biggest smile on her face, "Yes! Yes, I'll be honored to do it!"

The next morning, inside Coach Bradford's office, Sir sits across from his coach as he talks to the NCAA commissioner on speaker phone.

"You heard correctly," Coach Bradford says. "Sir is respectfully declining to come before the board."

"Then how does he expect to have a chance to get back on the court to play?"

"He doesn't feel comfortable sitting among the NCAA committee as if he's on trial being accused of something he didn't do."

"So, what does he want to do? We need to end this boycott."

"He's going to set up his own interview, via Facebook Live, answering any and all questions the appeals board wants answers to. I'm sure you have specific questions. Please send them to the interviewer and Sir will be sure to answer every one."

There's a long pause from the commissioner. Coach looks at Sir then shrugs.

"Are you there?" Coach Bradford asks.

"Where should we send the questions?" The commissioner reluctantly responds.

Sir smiles, pumping his fist.

"You can send all questions to the e-mail address alexmyles@howard.edu, and we'll let you know when to watch. Thank you." Coach hangs up the phone and gives a slight grin as he shakes his head, exhaling from the intense conversation. "You're something else, kid. I sure hope you know what you're doing."

At the news of Sir's decision, reporters and vloggers across the nation chime in on the story.

"After a week of NCAA athletes sitting down, the NCAA committee breaks traditional investigation protocol and grants Sir Walker an appeal..."

"In true millennial fashion, Sir has declined the hearing with the NCAA..."

"...Sir is deciding to be interviewed via Facebook live, technically allowing the world to be his court of opinion..."

"But ultimately, it still remains the NCAA's choice in deciding if he plays or not..."

"...that's if there's still a season to be played."

In a country club in one of the more upscale areas of Portland, there's a group of patrons sitting in the lounge area. It's unusually crowded for a weekday morning. Mr. Wakowski likes to gather with a few of his other retired colleagues from Nike for a round of golf when the greens are vacant.

"Petey," a man yells from the plaid and khaki pants group.

Mr. Wakowski glances through the crowd of men. Noticing that it isn't one of his regular, recognizable golf buddies calling his name, he walks closer. Over by the patio door next to a fireplace, a tall slender man with bright white hair is waiving him over. Mr. Wakowski immediately regrets that he made eye contact, making the man aware he heard and saw him. It is Michael Fisher. He and Mr. Wakowski started at Nike around the same time, and they always had a friendly rivalry as top sales performers with the company, so there was always a sense of competition between the two. After about a decade at Nike, Michael went to the Trailblazers as a marketing executive, however, the tension of their rivalry still remains whenever they share a room.

"How's retired life treating you?" Michael asks, gripping Mr. Wakowski's upper arm. "I spun in my chair 20 times when I heard you were getting out of the game, man!" They both share a laugh as Andy Williams, one of Mr. Wakowski's colleagues and golf buddies, walks toward them.

"Mike and Pete," Andy says. "Like the good ole days. If they did a 30 for 30 sales rival, you two would be Magic and Bird. Didn't know you were a member here."

"I'm not," Mike replies. "We are having our University of Oregon Athletics Alumni Luncheon today. We have to get our Ducks quacking again."

"What more do you guys need?" Mr. Wakowski asks. "You all have the best facilities; you got the swoosh…"

"Well, Petey," Michael interrupts. "When we're losing in-state All-Americans to HBCUs, we clearly don't have enough. How does that even happen?"

"We let Peter make his own decision," Mr. Wakowski fires back. "He's always been a smart and responsible kid, and Howard is a good institution. And looking at the season they are having, it seems like a promising choice."

"I've been following," Michael replies. "I see they have a little boycott going. Things could've been a lot simpler had he stuck with his own."

"His own?" Mr. Wakowski questions.

"Yeah Petey, his own in-state school." Michael replies while giving Mr. Wakowski another tap on the shoulder. "Don't get all self-righteous on me, Jesus."

He grabs Michael's hand and removes it from his shoulder, and the hostess approaches to inform them they are up next to take the tee.

"Your timing couldn't be better," Andy utters to the young lady amidst the awkward silence.

"Petey," Michael says in the background as Mr. Wakowski and Andy walk away, "there are rules to this thing. Tell that kid of yours don't make it harder than it has to be."

"Let it go man," Andy says to Mr. Wakowski. "He can't help who he is."

But Mr. Wakowski couldn't just let it go. "Is that the answer, Andy?" Mr. Wakowski replies. "It's just how he is? This is just how things work? Rules are the rules, right?"

"Pete, I didn't say that. I just think this thing has you worked up, and you may need to step back."

"Yeah, I do need to take a step back," Mr. Wakowski replies. "You know, when my son told me he would be going to Howard, I sounded exactly like Michael, and I'm now realizing I am a part of the problem. Following the rules and playing it safe is code for leaving things the way they have always been, whether someone is treated fairly or not." Andy stared back at Mr. Wakowski with a blank face and speechless. "I'm going to have to take a rain check on playing today," Mr. Wakowski continues. "Another time... Later."

Later that night, in his dorm room, Peter shifted in his bed. A still darkness covered the room with the exception of the bright orange numbers on his alarm clock. It's 1:23a.m. The pressure of the protest is growing his uneasiness by the minute as the thoughts of regret bounces around his head like a metal ball in a pin ball machine. Had he been at UCLA or Oregon, he'd be free of drama, cruising to the NCAA tournament and then the NBA Draft. *Did I overthink this thing?* He thought.

Light pierces from the edges of his iPhone as it lies face down vibrating. Peter has been keeping his phone on the other end of his room to prevent him from checking headlines and reading comments on Instagram and Twitter all night, but tonight, it's placed on his nightstand next to the bed. He turns it over to see a new message from his dad. Mr. Wakowski isn't a late-night phone guy, so Peter assumes he is either out at a bar drinking or something is on his mind.

"Son," the message reads, *"I know there has been sort of a wedge between us since you've been away at school, but I want to let you know I'm proud of you. Sometimes we have to see our off-base thinking through the words of others before we really understand the flaws in our ways. I was wrong. What you're doing takes a lot of guts, and your selflessness makes me even prouder to be your farther. Love you."*

Peter is stunned. His dad has always been stubborn, and going against him is not easy, so, to get through to him and get his vote of confidence lets Peter know he didn't make a mistake. Instantly, his uneasiness went away completely. Peter texted his dad back, *"I love you too."* Feeling a surge of belief, he immediately texts Earl and Sir, *"HBC-3*

Forever, we got this!"

Chapter 20 – The Interview

A chauffeur stands outside of a black SUV waiting for Alex to come outside of the dorm. She emerges from the doors, wrapped in a black peacoat, with her radiant, silky hair flowing from the bottom of her matching knitted beanie. The chauffeur greets her, opening the back door.

"Ms. Alexandria Myles?" he asks.

"Yes," she confirms.

"I'll be your escort to and from ESPN studios today."

"ESPN studios?" She asks, getting inside the car. "I thought we were just going to the workspace around the corner."

"I don't know anything about a workspace. I was instructed to take you to the studio where Mr. Walker awaits you."

She sits in the back of the SUV and texts Sir, *"ESPN studios?"*

He responds, *"Yep, I'll explain when you get here."*

Gazing at the stone architectures of the nation's capital from the tinted windows, a million things race through Alex's mind—specifically, what had transpired for them to be doing the interview, now, at the ESPN studio. She wonders if she is still the one interviewing, or if he is having her tag along because he initially asked her. She thinks how huge of an opportunity this is, regardless, if she has gotten the boot or not. She is going to the crème de la crème of sports networks, and surely, this is a blessing in itself. So, she is going to be overly prepared.

She begins reviewing the list of questions the board emailed her and the notes she made for specific questions. She practices her response to certain questions, and word pronunciations so she will come off as articulate as she can. She doesn't quite understand why Sir has chosen her to be a part of this experience, especially since she turned her back on him initially, but without a doubt, she is grateful.

As the makeup artist preps Alex for the camera, she feels euphoric—right at home. She has dreamed of this moment her whole life, and it is happening. She can't believe she is about to go on live television and conduct an interview concerning the nation's top sport's story. As the makeup artist blots her face, tears come to Alex's eyes just thinking about the occasion.

Not too long after she's there, Sir walks in the room. "What's up, big timer!" He calls out. "You ready?"

"All I have to do is ask the questions. You're the one in the hotseat. The question is, are you ready?"

"Lights. Cameras. Big stages. I've been doing this for a while now," he says with a smile. "All I have to do is tell my truth. Simple."

The producer of the show enters the room with a clip board in her hand and a pencil in her ear and says, "Sir, you're needed on stage for lighting."

"Okay, coming." He then turns back to Alex and says, "See you on stage. And by the way, you look beautiful." He gives her a wink, then, crosses toward the door, leaving the room.

Alex can't help but smile from ear to ear. The makeup artist smirks at the apparent love in the air.

"So, you're the reason he's doing this" the makeup artist enlightened.

"What do you mean?" Alex questions.

"You didn't hear? A bidding war happened yesterday, and ESPN won. ESPN offered him a million dollars toward a charity of his choice to do this interview. He declined. Instead the money is going toward scholarships for sports journalist majors attending HBCUs."

"Really?" Alex asks.

"Yep! Now I know why." She checks Alex's face for any imperfections, "You're all ready. Now go get'em girl," the makeup artist says encouragingly unsnapping the makeup cape from Alex's body.

In a pair of director's chairs, Alex and Sir sit across from one another in the dimly lit studio with a spotlight shining on just the two of them. Four cameras, strategically placed throughout the studio, catch them from all angles. They both display a bit of nervousness. Outside the camera's lens, Sir can't help but tap his crisp pair of Bred 11's on the leg of the chair, while Alex overly plays with the cap of the pen she's holding between her fingers. Alex may not be the one whose amateur career is on the line, but she knows she has just as much as Sir to gain from this interview, and she wants to come off as professional as possible.

She begins with a few warmup questions—questions about his mom, and where he's from, and about his friendship with the guys on the team. Questions to allow the nation to remember Sir's charming smile and his boyish All-American ways. They joke about the transition of going from a high schooler who depends on his parent for everything, to being an independent college freshman. It is easy to see the two of them have good chemistry and they are really just kids at heart, yet Alex displays full professionalism. After ten minutes or so, as instructed by the producer, Alex takes them to a commercial break.

"You two are doing great," says the producer, as Sir and Alex look at one another and exhale a little bit of anxiety they both have been holding on to. But because they know they are about to get into the nitty-gritty of things, a lot of the anxiety is still present.

The hair and makeup team give Alex and Sir their last looks and make sure they're flawless before they go back on air, Alex says, "Here we go…"

Sir responds, "I'll see you there," and nervously smiles.

"And five, four, three, two…" the producer counts down and then points to Alex, alerting her she's back on-air.

"So, you were saying earlier that your mom is a single parent who was in nursing school while you were in high school. How was that?" Alex asks.

"It was cool. She worked her butt off to provide as much as she could, though most of the money she made from her shifts at the restaurant went toward her tuition and books. We mostly only saw each other in the mornings as she made breakfast for me while studying and then at my games which she never missed. Any other time she was working or at school, and I was traveling and playing ball, trying to make it so she wouldn't have to work so hard."

"Well, you're a few months from being a top draft pick, if not the number one pick, so I'm sure your mom won't have to work that hard."

"It's who she is. She loves taking care of people. So, for her, that isn't work."

"Tell me about your family," Alex says.

"We don't have much. My grandfather, who played ball for Howard, passed away when I was about five. My grandmother died before I was thought of. They both were an only child, so not much family came from them. My mom has a brother who's in the military stationed overseas. So, we were pretty much on our own. Basketball was my family and still is."

"And who is Percy Daniels to you?"

Sir sighs, pausing for a second. Then with the nation watching on the edge of their seats, he answers, "Percy *was* like a dad to me. He made sure I had everything I needed. He protected me. He managed my life. He took care of me and my moms —paying for the things we couldn't, enabling her to not have to work as hard."

"So, you did take money from Mr. Daniels?" Alex asks.

"Yes, from the time I was in the sixth grade until I was a senior in high school, Percy was my main provider. But I never took any money from him nor anyone else to attend Howard. Nor did I take money to throw any games in high school, not even the state championship game."

"So, what did, in fact, happen in that championship game? Because from the outside looking in, it surely *looked* like it."

"The same thing that happened in my decision to choose Howard University to play. I didn't want to be a slave to the game of basketball anymore. I got tired of not being able to play the game freely as it was intended."

"Why do you feel as if you were a slave?"

Sir sighs. "Because I was. Because Percy took care of us, so I had to jump when he said 'jump' and run when he said 'run.'"

"What exactly did you have to do?" Alex asks, leaning forward.

"I just had to win games. And sometimes I had to win them big. That's what made me work harder than everyone else. A win wasn't a win unless I won how he needed me to win."

"Because Mr. Daniel's had money on those games?"

"Yup, tens of thousands. Sometimes more. Percy brought Vegas to Chicago high school basketball. And for four years, me and… I was his cash cow."

"Interesting," Alex says with a furrowed brow. "So, I know in betting sometimes it's worth more for the underdog to win. Did, you ever have to intentionally lose any games."

"Nope, never had to lose," he pauses. "Not until the state championship game." Sir stares off blankly into the studio.

"We'll be back after this commercial break," Alex says as they cut to commercial. "Are you okay?" She asks, putting her hand on Sir's, consoling him.

"Yeah, I'm cool," Sir says, snapping out of his blank stare and acknowledging her hand on his. "I just have to use the bathroom. I'll be back."

Inside the bathroom, Sir takes a deep look at himself in the mirror. He thinks about the information he has disclosed and what else he's about to tell. He doesn't want to reveal everything because he knows it could get Percy in a lot of trouble, and that's not what he wants for Percy. Percy was once his mans, the guy who had his back, who took care of him, made sure he never went without anything he needed. But his hand has been forced. Percy put him in a predicament he can't get out of unless he tells everything. He thinks, *"Yeah, I could just be quiet and go to the league and make my millions."* But that isn't the kind of guy he is. He thinks about the next wide-eyed young athlete that a guy like Percy would want to take advantage of and ruin. He thinks about how the world would see him as a liar and a cheater for the rest of his life if he didn't disclose the truth. Then, he concludes that he has to finish the interview. He has to finish telling his story. He splashes some water on his face, takes one last look in the mirror and says to himself, *"You got this."*

Now seated back in the studio, with the cameras rolling, Alex asks, "Before we went on break, you said you never had to lose a game, and you said you didn't throw the state championship game."

"I didn't. I lost the state championship game. My anger and my selfishness lost it for my team."

"Explain, please."

"We were up ten at the half and that's when Percy came to me and told me to throw the game. I didn't understand why he would want me to lose at something he knew I wanted to win so badly, but I agreed to do it because I felt I owed him my life. I was heartbroken, but, after all, he took care of me. And with my mom having one more semester of school, I didn't want her to have to stress and struggle through it worrying about cash because I didn't do my part. So, in the second half I started taking less shots, overpassing, and taking only shots that would keep the game close and make it look like I was trying to win still. Then it came to the point where Simeon caught up, and when it came down to losing the game, I couldn't actually go through with it. I wanted to *win*. And when we stole the ball in the final seconds of the game, all I could think was *exclamation point.* Nobody was going to tell me when I couldn't win. Ever! So, instead of holding the ball and allowing them to foul me, I just blanked out, and I drove to hole."

"And then what happened?" Alex asks.

"I say I was fouled, but the ref saw it differently. The defender blocked the ball. Next thing I know, I'm on the floor watching my boy, Rick, dunk the game winning basket for Simeon."

"I see… And how did you end up at Howard University from there?"

"After the game, I was so mad, and hurt, and upset, and confused. I decided that I didn't want anything else to do with Percy. It was clear to me that he no longer had my best interest at heart. And being that he was my connection to every top program that was recruiting me, I knew I had to break all ties with him. After having a talk with my great friend Booney and receiving Coach Bradford's recruitment letters, I decided that Howard was the place for me. And I asked Pete and Earl to join me. No longer a slave to the game. I made a choice for me. Chains broken."

With nothing more to say, Sir stares sincerely into Alex's eyes, raises his eyebrows and then lets out a deep breath through his nostrils. *Finally!* And Alex gazes back into his eyes and shares with him an innocent smile.

Back at the NCAA headquarters, reporters wait outside the boardroom where the commissioner and board members, having just watched Sir's interview, deliberate their decision. After an hour of waiting, the commissioner, garbed in a gray suit, comes out to address them.

"After careful deliberation, we believe Mr. Daniels' initial accusations against Sir Walker are false. We do not believe Sir accepted money to attend Howard University. Therefore, the NCAA has decided to absolve Sir of all allegations and repeal his suspension."

After hearing the news, within the walls of locker rooms, barbershops, living rooms, across the nation, fans and athletes go crazy, jumping for joy, hugging and high-fiving one another, reminiscent of Black America when Barack H. Obama won the 2008 presidential election becoming the first Black President of the United States of America.

"We did it," is the resounding statement heard from the student-athletes across the country.

"Will there be an NCAA tournament this year?" A reporter asks.

"Of course," the commissioner says. "We assume since we did our part, the student-athletes will now do theirs, and conference tournaments followed by Selection Sunday and then the NCAA tournament will resume this coming Thursday. Now, if you'll excuse me, we have a tournament to get back on track. Thank you."

Chapter 21 – Legacy

After ripping through their conference tournament and landing a number two seed in the NCAA Tournament, the Bison start their tournament against a number fifteen seed, right where they began their season—Madison Square Garden. They run through Abilene Christ University by thirty points, then, in the round of thirty-two, they smash on the tenth seed, Bradley University by twenty-two.

Though players of the opposing teams want to win, the vibe is different as rival players and fans show the Howard players the utmost love and respect—thanking them for banding together and having the courage to pioneer change.

The following weekend, the round of the Sweet Sixteen was must-watch TV in Washington D.C. at the Wizards' hometown arena. Having played all of their home games there this season, the Bison were right at home. Having home court advantage proved to be a huge upside for the Bison, as their fans made up more than eighty percent of the arena's attendance for their third and fourth round games. In the Sweet Sixteen, the Bison battled with third seed, Syracuse, the team that gave them their lone loss of the season, for most of the game. But in the final minutes, Howard, led by Sir's thirty-three-point night, pulled away, winning by eight. And in the Elite Eight, facing number one seeded Virginia, Howard walked away with the victory when Virginia couldn't make the game tying bucket at the buzzer.

No different from the start of the season, Howard University is the talk of the tournament and now the Final Four. HBCU pride is at an all-time high. Major brand companies and street vendors can't print up Howard and other HBCU paraphernalia fast enough. Of course, Black America has bought into the movement, but even White America has gotten in on it. After all, one-third of the HBC-3 is a white guy. The aforementioned aside, who doesn't love a winning basketball team, especially around tournament time?

Los Angeles is the host of the Final Four and the Bison are the biggest celebrities. A couple of hip-hop and pop stars are captured with Howard Final Four sweaters on. Even a few NBA and NFL stars wish them luck via Twitter. The attention the team is getting has quadrupled since the start of the season.

Sir, Peter, and Big Earl couldn't have imagined this—they or anyone else. The NCAA tournament has been around for decades, and "Cinderella" teams have made it plenty of times. Everybody loves an underdog story, but nothing like this has been seen before. Everyone knows who they are by now. Press conferences and practices are packed to capacity. Paparazzi follow them. Their hotel lobby is insane with people just waiting to catch a glimpse of them. Even on the streets of Venice Beach, where thousands of people hang out, palm trees sway in the wind, and big, beautiful blue waves wash along the shore, Howard's team is the main attraction, as people follow behind them, wishing them good luck and taking pictures with them. They are special, and the nation recognizes it.

For the HBC-3, making it to the Final Four had been a dream of theirs since they were little kids, just as any boy or girl who aspired to play college basketball. But for the rest of the team, the dream faded long ago. Dreams have become reality for them all, and they want to win. They know how much winning it all would mean for them, not only individually, but for

Howard University and HBCUs across the nation. An HBCU team has never gone this deep in the tournament, let alone been in contention to win an NCAA championship, so winning would put them right in line with the other elite basketball programs and on a path to greatness.

As the HBC-3 sit on the panel, still sweating from the game they've just played, a reporter asks, "Earl, having initiated The Sit Down in honor of your teammate, do you realize this moment would've never been a reality had the decision not been in your favor?"

"See, this is why I don't do interviews," Earl jokes, causing laughter all around. "But I've been doing boycotts since I was little, so I know that only two things could've resulted from it: We were gonna win now, or we were gonna win later," Earl shrugs. "This has been a God-ordained journey, and we came together for a reason bigger than we even realized initially. Once the devil stepped in and tried to derail what God orchestrated, is when I truly realized my part. So contrary to popular belief, I always knew The Sit Down would end in our favor. And come two days from now, when we face whoever we face in the national championship game, our God-ordained journey will be complete."

"Well said," Sir thinks to himself, nodding his head as he holds up his closed hand giving Earl a fist bump.

"March Madness is coming to a historic roller coaster finish with Chicago's very own Sir Walker and Rick Gray in the center of it," the local sports radio analyst says. *"The boycott from Sir's suspension at the end of the regular season, the NCAA reversal decision, and now he and his HBC-3 comrades are heading to the NCAA Championship game against Duke and Sir's best friend and high school rival, Rick Gray. This couldn't have been scripted better in a movie. Chicago wishes you well."*

Percy's SUV cruises as he forcefully changes the radio station before taking a tight pull of his cigar. A hard scowl covers his face. The foundation of what he built is in shambles at this point. He reminisces on his upbringing as a credible and sharp guy in the streets of Chicago but not able to pinpoint when he was forced to change. Until that state championship game, Sir has been like a son to him. The personal investment in Rick and Sir dates back before their adolescence. All that time and money lost can't go unanswered. He parks his car in front of the Jackson Park Recreation Center, fans off the cigar smoke, and heads into the gym.

From the long trophy case of summer and fall league champions to photos of guys that went on to play division-one college basketball and professionally, there is usually a pleasant sense of nostalgia meeting Percy when he walks through the doors of Jackson Park. Now, it only reminds him of the fall day he first laid eyes on a young Sir and Rick and the current state of their relationship. Sir always showed signs of veering off the path from day one, but Rick disconnecting from him cut him deeper. There was never a lack of trust or resistance of Percy's guidance from Rick. However, it was evident Rick's loyalty was stronger with Sir than it was with Percy because once Sir announced his point of no return with Percy, Rick soon followed.

He hasn't been to the gym in a while, but the odor, the squeaking gym shoes, and the young, hungry eyes of the ball players seem to make him feel right at home. "If it isn't the infamous Percy Daniels," a voice says from behind. "Surprised to see you here." Percy looks back to see Robert 'Squeaky' Mitchell, former high school basketball star, standing in the doorway of the custodian closet. He has been the janitor at the rec center for the last 20 years and is always willing to be a sound of wisdom or voice of reason for moments of conflict for teens in the area, which is often.

"Squeak, what's up my man?" Percy says. "Now why would it ever be a surprise for me to be here? This is home—always will be."

"Yeah, I know," he replies. "I just figured with the game being tomorrow, you'd be there rooting on the guys."

"Nope, not this time man. Not this time." Percy says somberly as he walks into the gym. "See you around, Squeak."

The gym is full of the usual—hustlers, local street guys, high school basketball coaches, and runners for agents. Everybody has a common interest in mind, which is getting their hands on or taking a controlling interest in some of the young talent in the gym. Percy walking in the gym epitomizes what the entire setting is about, as he is connected to everything involved, with the chatter about Sir and Rick being the pulse of the gym. Percy goes to his usual corner of the gym to observe. In usual circumstances, he'd be greeted by at least a coach and an agent that were salivating over some players he had in his back pocket, but today, he gets nothing but stares from afar.

"I got a lot riding on the game tomorrow, but I know Young Sir won't let me down," a distant voice exclaims from one of the bleachers.

"I wouldn't sleep on Rick. You remember the State Championship?" someone replies.

"I know who does remember," a loud domineering voice says from the group of guys. "Ain't that right, Percy? I lost twenty-five stacks that day, and this fool had the audacity to sit up on National TV to snitch and brag about how he was fixing games with Rick and Sir."

"That's right, Big Mike," Percy says. "I had the game in my pocket, and it's been that way for a long time. Some guys win and some get played, but the game is the game. Now, are you gonna cry about it or handle your business?"

The gym grows quiet. Percy was not a dude to mess with, but Big Mike sensed him weakening. He lost his kids and lost the respect of the streets, so his usual aura is lacking.

"Yeah, you played me and a bunch of others," Mike replies. "But look at you now? You got outsmarted by some kids, and you a snitch. So, what you got now?"

Percy approaches Mike, a six-feet, nine-inches, three hundred pound bruiser. The eye contact didn't slip once. "A bunch of kids will never play me," Percy says. "Unlike you, when I feel like I'm getting played, I do something about it. You think they are going to take my money and rob my enterprise and live to talk about it? You and the rest of these clowns got it confused if you think they're going to run off with their lives and forget what I did for them and their families."

Mike takes a step toward Percy, leaving only air and an opportunity for a chin shot. "You stand here and think you're holding court like a man and calling us clowns, but you're the clown," Mike says. "You're going on and on about who disrespected you, and you got your chest poking out about what you're about to do to some kids from this community because they got hip to the game you were running on them but fronting like you're an OG." Mike grinds his teeth and squints his eyes. "You're done around here and anywhere else. You won't get your hands on another kid in this neighborhood." Mike pulls up the bottom of his shirt and flashes the chrome pistol tucked in the waist of his size forty-eight jeans. "And if Sir or Rick get as little as a threat from you, you're a dead man."

Percy glances down then back up at Mike. "What, am I supposed to be scared, cause you got a little heater on you?" he sarcastically says, not shying away from an altercation. "You know my pedigree, and we can definitely turn this into a Navy Pier Fourth of July fireworks show."

"Yeah, we can," Mike responds, stepping back and now standing side by side with several others, showing there's strength in numbers. "But just know, this will be a firework show that ain't gonna have you clapping in the end."

Percy looks into the eyes of the others, realizing they all are in agreement with Mike. Percy takes a takes a step back, and throws up his hands, while devilishly smirking. "Y'all got it. I'll see y'all around."

"Not before, we'll see you," Mike fires back.

Percy takes a few steps back. He then takes a good look around the gym, and finally, his defeated eyes lock in on a kid. He has to be in sixth or seventh grade, with long arms and athletic build. The kid looks back at

Percy and then runs to the other end of the court. He's wearing a Howard

University jersey with the name Walker on the back. "Damn," Percy thinks

to himself shaking his head, then slides out the side door.

Lights! Camera! Action! The drums and horns of the Howard

University band are heard as they play a resounding upbeat tune,

electrifying the crowd, standing on their feet watching as the Bison of

Howard and the Blue Devils of Duke warm up on the court, preparing to

face off in the NCAA championship game.

Off to the side of half-court with the two teams in their

background, lights and cameras capture a panel of well-dressed

sportscasters reporting the action. *"We are minutes away from what we'd*

like to call a very historic season," a sportscaster enthusiastically says

after the return from commercial break. *"After an unprecedented chain of*

events in the NCAA, we are about to see first time contenders, the number

two seeded Howard Bison, face-off against the glorified and overall

number one seeded Duke Blue Devils for the NCAA National

Championship."

"Unprecedented is correct," another sportscaster chimes in. *"The Howard Bison have made believers out of the world that anything is possible, landing three All-Americans, reaching number five in the country, leading an NCAA boycott, tearing through the NCAA tournament, and now playing for the national championship. I'm excited!"*

"I'm excited too! The Howard Bison, led by the HBC-3—Walker, Singleton and Wakowski—up against the Blue Devils team that has been collectively devouring opponents. But since the start of the tournament, the freshman sensation, Rick Gray, has been leading the host of talented All-Americans. This game should be what the fans have been waiting for."

After the conclusion of the National Anthem, the crowd cheers fanatically, and the players take to their respected huddles. It's apparent that everyone is a tad bit nervous, even the coaches. After all, it is the national championship. Nevertheless, Coach Bradford is enthused.

"This is it guys. In my mind we're already champions, but that doesn't mean we don't have to go out here and give it our all." Coach Bradford pauses. "I just want to let you all know that I'm very proud of each and every one of you. You all are true men of courage and honor to the game of basketball and to this whirlwind we call life. I thank you all for helping me become a better coach as well as a better person. Now, let's go out here and win this game! Big Earl..." He says as they all gather their hands in the middle of the huddle.

"We've been at battle all year, fellas," Earl says, "On the court and off of it. It has been nothing short of a war for us. So tonight, we're approaching this as the last battle of the war, and I need to know that y'all are ready. So, when I ask y'all if y'all are ready, I need you to assure yourselves by responding, 'Let's go!'" Earl looks at his fellow teammates nodding their heads and bellows out the chant, "Hoop squad, hoop squad, ready to go to war?"

"Let's go!" they all yell in unison.

As the starters for each team cross onto the court, Duke's coach stops Rick by casually placing his hand on his shoulder and saying into his ear, "That was a good thing you did in standing up for your friend and the rights of student-athletes, but this is why you came to Duke... to be a champion. Time to get you a ring, young man." With pure focus in his eyes, Rick nods then proceeds onto the court.

Lining up for the jump-ball next to Sir, reminiscent of their high school battles, Rick says, "Just cause I protested with y'all, don't mean I'm about to take it easy on y'all."

"I don't expect you to," Sir responds, smiling. Rick smiles back.

Jump ball! Howard wins the tip.

"And this year's NCAA championship is on its way," the commentator says.

As Sir runs the show, the ball finds its way into the post. Earl pounds into the Duke defender then slams the ball over his head. The Staple's Center goes crazy as fans jump to their feet.

"My, oh my! What a way to start off a game," the commentator exclaims.

Ecstatically, Duke's coach jumps off the bench and gives it to the refs early. "Was that not an offensive foul?" he shouts with his hands thrown up.

"Good no-call, ref," Coach Bradford yells out then looks to his assistants. "At least he's consistent," he says remembering him from their very first game when he pleaded to the same ref to make the call for Big Earl.

The Blue Devils bring the ball up the court. Rick cuts up to the wing.

"Gray curls off the screen. He floats it up. Swish! And we are all even at two," the commentator reports.

"It might be a long night," Rick talks trash to his good friend.

With Rick guarding him, Sir dives through the lane without the ball.

"Touch pass from Walker to Wakowski... He nails the three!" The commentator says.

Talking a little trash back, Sir says, "I hope you know we're just getting started."

A few plays later, with the Bison leading 10-6, Sir jumps the passing lane. *"Walker with the steal and the jam!"* The commentator exclaims.

Joy, Sir's mother, jumps from her seat, excited with the rest of the crowd, as the Duke coach calls for a timeout.

The guys at Prince Jones Barbershop high-five each other watching the game and rooting on their hometown team.

"Don't look like he's throwing this game," Pops says.

"Hell naw, it don't," another barber agrees.

"We have to stay patient on both ends of the court and they'll give us whatever we want," Coach Bradford says to his team during the timeout.

"We are Duke University. We've been here before, yet we're playing like we haven't. We should be up at least ten points. This is uncharted territory for that program. I don't care who they have," the coach chastises his team. "We have to play like we care about that name across our chests, because they sure as hell are."

A few plays later, Rick goes up for the alley-oop dunking all over Eric. "And one!" Rick yells in Eric's face.

"Get out my face!" Eric yells in response to Rick's gloating.

"What you wanna do?" Rick fires back.

As the teams have to separate the two, the ref blows his whistle issuing double technical fouls.

"Gray and Sanders have both been hit with technical fouls and neither coach is happy," the commentator reports.

"You have to stay calm out there, son. Don't give them a reason to put you out this game," Coach Bradford stresses.

"But he was all up in my face," Eric responds, in a childlike manner.

"I know, but we need you out there."

Duke's coach leans over to his assistants and says, "At least somebody is playing with some intensity out there."

After a hard-fought first half of play, Duke leads forty-two to forty with eight seconds remaining in the half. Sir comes off a screen, receiving the ball in the short corner. With the defender on him, Sir rises up for the shot.

"Walker nails the shot at the buzzer," the commentator exclaims. *"And we are all tied at the half. Wait, Walker is down."*

The cheers for the shot instantly turn into gasps around the arena as the crowd watches Sir squirming on the floor, grabbing at his ankle. A dead silence fills the arena.

"It appears as if he came down on the defender's foot. This doesn't look good for the Bison," the commentator reports.

Inside the Bison locker room, the players sit around with their heads hung low, worried about their teammate, while Sir lays stretched out on the trainer's table, getting his ankle examined. Coach Bradford approaches.

"How bad is it?" Coach Bradford asks, with great concern.

"On a scale of one to ten… about a seven," the trainer responds. Coach Bradford scratches his head.

"So, he's done for the night?" Coach asks, already sure of the answer.

"That's entirely up to you and him."

"Look, I don't want you to go back out there if it means making it worse. You've got a promising career ahead of you. You've done more than enough for this school and program," Coach says.

"How bad do you need me?" Sir asks.

"On a scale of one to ten… about a fifteen," Coach jokes. They all laugh. "But we've managed without you before."

As the clock ticks, Sir thinks about what he and Earl talked about when he was lying in bed in the hospital. "Coach you mind grabbing Earl for me?"

"Sure," Coach says, leaving out.

Earl enters the room with Coach, "You rang?" He asks.

"Yeah… looks like I'm gonna need a minor miracle Big Fella. You mind?" He says, extending his hand.

"Say no mas," Earl replies, grabbing Sir's hand and beginning to pray: "Our Father who art in Heaven…" While Earl prays for Sir, the trainer begins to wrap Sir's ankle in athletic wrap.

With about two minutes remaining on the clock until the start of the second half, Duke's coach calls his players in from warming up. "Now I'm not sure if Sir is going to play or not but we still have to play our game. Duke basketball is what's got us here, and Duke basketball is what's going to win this game for us," he says. Just as he finishes his statement, the crowd roars as the Bison come running out of the tunnel, led by Sir. "Well it looks like we're going to have the privilege of defeating them with Sir on the floor."

Just before the buzzer sounds, the two coaches sell their teams on what they're going to do to put themselves in position to win the game:

"Twenty minutes fellas. Twenty minutes of giving it your absolute all, is all I'm asking for. If we go out there and give everything that we have, in twenty minutes we'll be crowned champions," Coach Bradford instills in his players.

"Now they think they're going to ride off in the sunset on our behalf, with our championship. But boy are they wrong," Duke's coach reiterates.

"They're going to try to attack Sir's ankle. Test it at all cost. But we're a team and we're going to protect his ankle as much as we can," Coach Bradford informs his players.

And as if Coach Bradford were in Duke's coach's head, on queue, Duke's coach informs his players, "I want to test Sir's ankle. If he's guarding you, you go at him. We're going to pick and roll and backdoor cut him to death, making sure he's in every defensive play. This is our game. Now let's go out there and get this 'W'! Win on three. One, two, three..."

"Win!" is heard from both huddles simultaneously as the second half buzzer sounds.

The second half of action is under way and Duke starts out with the first possession. The point guard dribbles up the court and calls out the play.

"It's going to be interesting to see what the Blue Devils do to try and break loose from these Bison," the commentator says.

Immediately a Duke player backdoor cuts to the basket for two points, leaving Sir stuck, standing still. The following possession, Howard shoots and misses. The ball is rebounded and quickly outlet. The Duke player catches it and blows past Sir leaving him, once again, stuck on his heels.

"Way to run," Duke's coach says, clapping to encourage his team. Coach Bradford paces the sideline with a look of concern, early.

A few possessions later, Rick does a step back move on Sir and pulls up for two. *Swish!*

"And that's another back-to-back scoring on Walker who seems to be favoring his ankle pretty early," the commentator points out. *"The Blue Devils now lead by eight."*

It's easy to see that Sir is not himself—moving very gingerly—almost afraid to make any sudden moves on defense. And it's getting him killed out there. Down fifty-six to forty-eight, Sir shows a sign of his competitive nature by driving to the basket the next play down, drawing a foul plus the basket.

"And one! What a move by Walker who seems to have landed awkwardly on that ankle," the commentator emphasizes, as Sir hobbles toward the Bison's bench. Howard fans gasp once again at the sight of this.

Coach Bradford meets Sir as he approaches. "That's a hell of a move kid, but I can't allow you to continue like this. I'm pulling you out after this free throw," he says.

"Nah, Coach. I'm good," Sir pleads with puppy dog like eyes. "Just trust me. I ain't done yet."

Stuck between a rock and hard place of taking a chance on the gimpy player that got him to this point or watching his best player go down, fighting is Coach Bradford's dilemma. But every great coach knows, if your best player says trust him, then that's what you do.

Coach Bradford reluctantly responds, "All right, kid. Be careful." Sir then limps back out on the court and knocks down the free throw.

On Duke's next possession, they go right at Sir, once again. The player gets the step on Sir, but he taps the ball from behind. Peter retrieves it then throws it up ahead to Sir who lays it in for two. This sparks a little run for the Bison as they collectively defend better and get a few more easy buckets.

The two teams go back and forth scoring and making one great play after another while the coaches counter each other with great plays like seasoned chest players. The game is intense, and the players are playing their hearts out, leaving it all on the line just as their coaches have asked. And with a minute and thirty-one seconds left on the clock, Earl sets a backdoor screen for Tommy who catches the alley-oop from Sir and slams it home. This gives Howard their first lead of the second half. Duke's coach has seen enough and calls a timeout.

"This isn't a place we haven't been before. We've been down, but you can never count us out. We are Duke. And we always find a way to win," he says, pensively staring into the eyes of his young men.

"They think they're going to take this moment from us, but no way. This moment is ours because we want it more. We've always wanted it more," Coach Bradford says to his guys.

"This is uncharted territory for them. That's why in a minute and thirty-one seconds we will be victorious. Do you understand me?" Duke's coach asks his players.

"Yes sir," they resoundingly answer.

"You all have been in this moment before. Maybe not in reality, but you've dreamed about it at least a thousand times, acting it out in your backyards walking away with the feeling of a champion. Now it's time to make those dreams a reality. You all go out there and execute in this last minute and thirty-one seconds, and you'll be able to call yourselves basketball's first HBCU NCAA National Champions," Coach Bradford preaches to his players who are locked in on his every word—firing them up. "Let me hear you say 'Champions' on three. One, two, three..."

"Champions!" The Howard players scream out.

The starters for the Howard Bison take to the court for what is probably their final time together. Sir leads them with Peter and Earl slightly behind him, and Eric and Tommy slightly behind them, embodying the classic "V" formation of geese in flight. Just as birds are able to fly higher in the updraft created by the lead bird, this group of young men have been able to do the same—fly high—because of Sir's leadership. They came together, to soar freely without restriction, and play the game they love. They didn't know what was going to come of the journey they set out to explore, but they did know that whatever it was going to be, they had to do it together. With a minute and thirty-one seconds remaining, in addition to hard work and sacrifice, together, they've put themselves in the position to be crowned with collegiate athletics' ultimate honor. There is no denying what they are feeling. The look in each one of their eyes says they are ready for the moment.

"Duke sets it up, working their offense. Gray gets it off the curl," the commentator says as Rick catches the ball. *"He shoots the floater. He scores. And we're tied at sixty-eight."*

Afterwards, Sir brings the ball up the court and calls out the play with the defender's wings spread wide and applying intense pressure. There's some bumping of their bodies, but not enough for the ref to call a ticky-tack foul.

"The Bison show patience as they look for a shot. A down screen is set for Wakowski," the commentator says as Peter catches it in the short corner. *"And he nails it! Putting the Bison up by two."*

From the stands, Mr. Wakowski, wearing an HBC-3 shirt, high-fives his wife. "Great shot, son," he says clinching his jaw and pumping his fist.

The next possession down, Sir takes the responsibility of guarding Rick who has the ball. The Bison send the double-team.

"Gray picks up his dribble, but quickly finds Johnson cutting to the basket," the commentator reports. *"And he banks it in! And we're knotted at seventy with thirty-six seconds remaining."*

Immediately after the bucket, Coach Bradford screams for his team to push it. Sir pushes the ball up the court, finding Eric who pump fakes and drives to the hole. The defender steps up, and he underhand passes it to Earl for the slam.

"That's my son," Mr. Singleton proudly shouts with his chest poked out to those around him, as if they don't already know.

"And the Bison respond with an easy score from Singleton. And with twenty seconds remaining and down two, the Blue Devils don't have a timeout, so they need to get a good quick shot."

With the crowd on their feet and the players standing damn near on the court to see the action from the bench, Duke's coach screams for his team to push it as everyone watches Rick burst up the court, with Sir applying the pressure. Duke works the ball around. Twelve seconds remain. Rick comes off the down-screen, with Sir trailing him. The ball is thrown to Rick and with ten seconds remaining, Sir jumps the lane.

"The ball is knocked loose!" the commentator yells.

As the ball sails toward the sideline, Sir saves it before it goes out of bounds, flinging it over Rick's head, to Eric breaking downcourt.

"Walker to Sanders! Six seconds! Gray trails. Sanders back to Walker..."

Sir catches the ball with four seconds on the clock. His adrenaline is shooting through his body like a live wire, forgetting his injured ankle. He takes flight, soaring high before Rick has a chance to jump with him. *Slam!*

"Oh my! Oh my! Walker slams it! The Bison win! The Bison win! The Howard Bison are your NCAA National Champions," the commentator shouts at the top of his lungs as the crowd goes crazy and Howard players rush the floor, tackling Sir, and piling on top of him as they share tears of joy.

Coach Bradford, overwhelmed by the surreal moment, takes a seat on the bench and stares blankly into space. So filled with emotion, he needs a minute to breathe. An emotional Mia watches her husband from the stands in his moment as tears of joy roll down her cheeks.

After an extensive celebration with his teammates, Sir breaks away from the crowd and finds his mother in the stands. She blows him a kiss and mouths, "I'm so proud of you!"

He shakes his head and mouths back, "Nah, I'm proud of us!" He smiles and winks then goes to find his coach. As he turns, Rick is standing there with his hand extended. The two of them shake up and pull one another in for the hug.

"I'm proud of you, bro," Rick says. "You deserve this moment. You always have. And I can't thank you enough for not mentioning me being involved with P."

"Thank you, bro," Sir responds. "You know that ain't even my style."

"I know it's not. Enjoy your moment. We'll rap. And we'll definitely continue this thing on the next level. Brothers for life."

"Fa sho'! Brothers for life," Sir repeats back as he and Rick part ways.

"We did it, Coach. We did it," Sir says standing above Coach Bradford, still seated on the bench.

Coach Bradford raises his head, and with his eyes full of tears, he looks up to see that it's Sir, and he says, "No. You did it, son. You did it." He rises to his feet and pulls Sir in for a big hug as confetti rains on them from the rafters and the Howard band plays, *Hey* by Gary Glitter. Not much long after, here come Earl and Peter singing along wearing their championship hats and shirts with a matching pair for Coach Bradford and

Sir. Sir throws on his hat and shirt, and he and Coach join in on the song. "Dun, dun, dun, nunna, nuh, hey! Dun, dunna, nuh…"

In the midst of their celebration, Alex's idol and world-renowned sports journalist, Lisa Salters, approaches with a mic in-hand. "Sir, can we grab you for second?" She asks.

"Sure," he says. "But first there's somebody I'd like you to meet. Sir takes her by the hand, and escorts her to where Alex is standing. Alex's eyes widen with excitement, when she sees Sir approaching, waving her towards them. "Miss Salters, I'd like you to meet my girl, Alex. Alex, meet Miss Lisa Salters."

"Hi," Alex shyly says.

"Hey sweetheart," Lisa says. "I loved your interview."

Alex stands stiff as a board, jaw dropped at knowing her idol knows who she is.

A few weeks later, in a small tattered high school gymnasium in Brooklyn, New York, the number one ranked high school basketball player sits at a table before reporters and flashing cameras. After a heartwarming speech, he says to the world, "After careful consideration, it is my honor to follow in the footsteps of a group of courageous athletes before me." He puts on a Howard Bison baseball cap, and concludes, "Next season, I too will attend the HBCU Howard University and play for Coach Bradford and the Bison."

Over the next few hours, announcements from the nation's top high school basketball players start pouring in. To the country's surprise, not just Howard receives commitments, but other HBCUs receive some as well. Guaranteed to be NBA lottery picks, Sir, Peter and Earl have proven that it's not the school that makes the athletes, but the athletes who make the school. All it took was for a few individuals to believe in each other and themselves and believe they were enough to make a difference for change. And that's what they did. They changed the game instead of becoming slaves to it.

Chains broken.

ACKNOWLEDGEMENTS

First and foremost, I'd like to thank my Lord and Savior for giving me the words to say and the resources enabling me to make this story possible. I wrote a Facebook post over a year ago congratulating my friend, Frank, on the completion of his book, and I told my boy, Rick, that he was up next. My mother replied to the post, basically telling me I was next, too. I had no intentions of writing a book at that time, so I thank my mother for planting that seed before I even knew it existed. Love you, Momma! My family and my close friends are the inspiration for anything I do, so I thank you all for the motivation. We all we got! Some of the characters in the book are named after actual people in my life, and that's my way of saying thank you for being who you are or who you were to me. You've had more influence on my life than you know, and I appreciate who you are. It takes a village, and I am definitely a true product of a great one. From my Gran, to my Papa, to my parents, my siblings, and beyond. I thank you all. Ro, you killed that monologue, bro! Thank you. Jaecob, Biggah, Colin… my man

Ed—we gotta another one! And Adrian, you bodied the cover! You all played intricate parts to getting this project done, and I can't thank you guys enough. My Godmother, Bootsie, who's always praying for me has been sending me messages for the past year asking me what I would like her to pray for specifically, and I always say the success of this book. And I know it's because of those specific prayers that this book will be great. While writing this book, I reached out to several folks to help with the marketing campaign, so I want to thank you guys for taking the time and posting the cover of this book on my behalf. Thank you!! To Shortie & Kdub, I can't thank you guys enough for always having my back. Since my college years or before, you ladies have been editing my papers and most times doing more than asked. It's an ongoing joke between us that you each own a third of my college degree for the help you've provided to me, and this book is no different. Taking the time out of your busy schedules, even while pregnant and raising kids, you found the time to do what you've always done for ya boy. Friends for life. And I love you both. To CB, keep grinding, my dude. The coach was named after you because that's what you are. A coach. You have so much insight about life and the game of basketball that this character is how I see you—someone destined for greatness. To my man Boon, when I was thinking of the character name for whom I think is the most important character in this story, it was a no brainer that I was going to name him after you. The knowledge that you've gifted me with since I was teenager, I can't thank you enough for. And naming this character after you, is my way of saying I respect you; I love who you've been to me and thank you for being a positive God-fearing male role model in my life. Every young guy should have a "Booney" that they can look up to. Last, but not least, to my boy Rick who I named a character after from its inception but came on in the rewrites to add more beauty, life, and insight to the story. The story wouldn't be what it is without you and I can't thank you enough. That's why I felt it was only right to add your name to the cover as well. We in this together, and I thank you for believing in me, bro. To everyone that purchased, read, and passed on info about this book—THANK YOU! And GODSPEED! 🙏

SLAVE TO THE GAME MERCHANDISE

Shop these products and more at 1140Productions.com

Made in the USA
Middletown, DE
28 July 2020